DEEP SHOCK

Sunday passed quietly, much to everyone's relief, especially those in the law enforcement field. Doc Williams released the bodies of Ruth Jordan and Barbara Hartman for burial. It was a double funeral. The funeral of Joy Grotin Pike would be held Tuesday.

Monday afternoon, just after the girls' funerals, a small package arrived at the home of Howard and Sissy Jordan.

Sissy's screaming brought her husband on the run. He had not yet returned to his office, and their only surviving child was at the home of a friend.

His wife was alternating between incoherent babbling and wild screaming. She stood pointing at a box.

Inside it was a newspaper photo of Judy Evans.

BOOK YOUR PLACE ON OUR WEBSITE AND MAKE THE READING CONNECTION!

We've created a customized website just for our very special readers, where you can get the inside scoop on everything that's going on with Zebra, Pinnacle and Kensington books.

When you come online, you'll have the exciting opportunity to:

- View covers of upcoming books
- Read sample chapters
- Learn about our future publishing schedule (listed by publication month *and author*)
- Find out when your favorite authors will be visiting a city near you
- Search for and order backlist books from our online catalog
- Check out author bios and background information
- Send e-mail to your favorite authors
- Meet the Kensington staff online
- Join us in weekly chats with authors, readers and other guests
- Get writing guidelines
- AND MUCH MORE!

Visit our website at
http://www.pinnaclebooks.com

BLOOD OATH

William W. Johnstone

Pinnacle Books
Kensington Publishing Corp.

http://www.pinnaclebooks.com

PINNACLE BOOKS are published by

Kensington Publishing Corp.
850 Third Avenue
New York, NY 10022

Pinnacle and the P logo Reg. U.S. Pat. & TM Off.

First Printing: September, 1999
10 9 8 7 6 5 4 3 2 1

Printed in the United States of America

For all we take we must pay, but the price is cruel high.

Rudyard Kipling

From the transcript of a Sheriff's Department taped interview.

June, 1999

"You have to believe me. No one among us meant the initiation to turn violent. Not at first, that is. God! It never had before. It was . . . well, spontaneous. Just got out of hand so quickly no one seemed able, or willing, to stop it. But I'm glad that it's finally, finally over. Dear God. Brought to light. I'm—all of us—those that are left whole, that is, are so tired of living with this shame, this secret. But, why did—I mean—why the kids? Why now, after all these years? Why this awful thing?

"Oh, Lord! It just got out of hand, that's all. None of us meant it. If only that girl hadn't started crying and fighting. If only her brother hadn't taken things so seriously and tried to fight the boys. God! It was so long ago. I don't know . . . it's all so hazy in my mind. But I remember we all went a little crazy, and his actions just seemed to push the boys over the line."

Lt. Davis: "Tell me what happened that night."

"It was the summer of nineteen seventy-three. A beautiful night. So lovely. We were between Denton and Red Bay, just inside the park—"

Lt. Davis: "What park?"

"Eureka Park. Right along the shore of Bell Lake. You know, where we all have our lodges. But we were some distance from them. It was just a silly kid initiation, that's all. We called it the Club of the Elite. You know, that's what a lot of people called our parents: The Elite Eleven. You remember the club, don't you, Joe?"

Lt. Davis: "Yes, I've heard of it. I remember it."

"We never asked you to join, did we?"

Lt. Davis: "Go on with your story, please."

"You never liked us, did you, Joe? And you still don't like any of us very much, do you? You thought we were all too wild, didn't you? Too much money and freedom. Oh, you were always the proper one, weren't you?"

No response from Lt. Davis.

"And you really never liked me especially, did you? Come on, admit it."

No response from Lt. Davis.

"Sure, sure. I know. We were the rich kids from the Hill Section, and you were the poor kid from the wrong side of town. Same old story, different writer. But I never snubbed you. Did I? I was never mean or ugly to you. Was I?"

Lt. Davis: "It is not my job to engage in personalities. Just tell me what happened back in nineteen seventy-three. You wanted this meeting, remember?"

"I have to go to the bathroom."

Lt. Davis: "Out the door and to your right, just down the hall."

"Aren't you coming with me?"

Lt. Davis: "I think you can manage by yourself."

(Approximately a four minute delay in recording.)

"I have a question. Are you going to pick up all the others?"

Lt. Davis: "I don't know. Probably so. Depends on what you tell me."

"How is my husband?"

Lt. Davis: "He has been taken to the psychiatric ward at Denton General."

"I see. I've decided I want my lawyer present."

Lt. Davis: "That is your right. You have not been charged with any crime, and you have admitted, on tape and in the presence of a police stenographer, that the statements you have given were given voluntarily and of your own free will."

"I still want my lawyer."

Lt. Davis: "I heard that."

Prologue

June, 1973

"I'm scared, Paul," the girl admitted to her twin brother in a whisper. "I just don't like any of this. I want to go home."

He shushed her and attempted to allay her fears, even though he had fears of his own. "It's just a game, kind of. They're just trying to scare us. Nothing is going to happen to us—not really. No one is going to hurt you, Judy."

I hope, he thought.

The girl was not convinced, and her hand trembled as she took her brother's hand. "If you say so, Paul. But I don't wanna undress down to my panties. That's not nice. Something might happen that we don't wanna happen."

They were the youngest ever to be initiated into the Club of the Elite. Paul and Judy Evans were thirteen.

"I don't know." Her brother snickered

softly, looking around the circle of young boys and girls. "I'd kinda like to see some of these girls without their clothes."

"Paul!" she admonished. "Think what Mother and Daddy would think. That's a dirty thing to say."

Then an older boy stood before them. He was sixteen, and he looked at Judy with open lust. He had mean eyes, Paul observed. And he was half drunk, and half naked.

"Take off your jeans and shirt," he told Judy. "You, Paul, down to your shorts."

Paul had seen the look in the boy's eyes change as he gazed at Judy, and Paul was wary of this. He felt he and his sister had made a mistake coming here this night. "And if we do that," he asked. "What next?"

The older boy shrugged his big shoulders.

"You take the oath, drink the eagle's blood, you're admitted, and then we all go for a swim in the lake."

"That's it?" Paul questioned.

"That's it. No big deal at all. Of course," the older boy said, grinning, "if you're both chicken. . . ?"

Paul slipped out of his jeans and shirt, a painfully thin boy. His ribs were outlined in the flames from the open fire on the shores of Bell Lake. A fish leaped from the water, smacking on impact. A bird called a lonely cry. The wind hummed through the thick timber, sighing a wistful cry.

I don't like this, Paul thought. *I just don't like this at all. Something is wrong. Something is going to happen here tonight. I ought to grab Judy's hand and run away.*

But he did not. Instead, he pushed the youthful premonition of danger from his mind and stood half naked in the center of the circle.

In that circle of boys and girls, a girl giggled at him, and Paul was embarrassed. He glanced at the source of the giggle and saw the girl was clad only in bra and panties. Paul was further embarrassed when he felt an erection begin to grow. The girl's eyes were riveted on his crotch. She raised her eyes to his and licked her lips.

Paul stuck out like a stiff banner.

Judy slowly undressed, shyly. Paul wanted to yell at her, to tell her to hurry up and get it done! She was being very provocative in her slowness, and the older boy was breathing kind of funny, his eyes on Judy's tiny breasts. She wore no bra, and her developing nipples were jutting out from fear and excitement. The older boy's erection was plain, and large.

Then Paul began to slowly relax as the older boy moved back into the circle and the shadows. The brother and sister took the oath—kind of a silly oath, really—and they were accepted into the very secret Club of the Elite. They were then asked to drink from the sacred cup. They were told it was eagle's blood, but neither of them believed that. They knew it was vodka and grape juice, but in the semi-darkness, around the flickering fire, the stuff did kind of resemble blood. It was good-tasting; cold and tingly going down. And it made them both feel good: lightheaded and relaxed. They each had several cups of the mixture.

"To the lake!" someone shouted. "Everyone to the lake for a dip."

Someone turned on a portable radio and the night was filled with music and laughter.

The boys and girls were all in various stages of intoxication, and they all had to go home pretty soon, so a dip in the cold waters of Bell Lake seemed like a pretty good idea: it would sober them up.

On the banks of Bell Lake an older girl shoved another cup of eagle's blood in Paul's hand. He drank it and was falling-down drunk in minutes. After a very short swim in the lake, the boys and girls paired off, Paul finding himself with an older girl. He couldn't help his condition; he had a full erection just looking at her, with everything she had wetly outlined. She pulled him to the cool bank and kissed him on the mouth, running her tongue over his lips.

"Do me," she said, her breath hot and sweet on his face. "Do me!"

"What?" Paul did not have the faintest idea what she wanted. Surely she didn't mean *That!*"

"Do it to me," she said, running her fingers across his wet belly.

"I . . . I don't know what you mean. What do you want me to do?"

"God, you kids are stupid! Don't you know anything? Here, let me show you. It feels good." She pulled off her panties and then helped Paul out of his underwear shorts. She grasped his erection and pumped him for several seconds, while she took his hand and placed it between her legs.

"Just use your fingers," she instructed him. "Ah! Right there. That's it. Play with me and I'll do you. We don't really do anything bad, just play around a little bit. Don't that feel good to you, Paul?"

Paul admitted, chokingly, that what she was doing to him did feel good.

But Paul's first experience at sex was cut short by a scream from his sister. He tried to push the girl from him, but she refused.

"You can't leave me like this!" she protested. "I'm almost at the good point, damn you!"

"Paul," Judy screamed. "Paul! Help me!"

The boy summoned all his strength and

pushed the older girl from him. He jumped to his feet, running toward the sound of his sister's screams. Someone laughed in the darkness, then tripped Paul. He fell hard on the ground, smashing his nose and lips on a log. Waves of nausea flooded him, and he was sick on the ground. He lay dazed and hurt for a few moments, his sister's screams faint in his ears, as if coming from a far place. It seemed unreal to him, a dream turned into a nightmare. The nightmare filled with real blood and pain and cries for help.

Paul crawled painfully to his feet, aware that his knees were torn and bleeding. His mouth and nose hurt, and he felt dizzy and sick. He could not understand why all the others were laughing, and why no one wanted to help his sister. Perhaps, he thought, his sister was just acting, this was all part of the initiation.

But he knew it was real when he spotted Judy, only a few yards away, on the ground, on her back, her pale naked legs spread wide, the older boy who had looked at her lustily between her legs, pushing in and out in a humping movement. Judy was screaming while the other kids, boys and girls, laughed drunkenly.

"Get off!" a boy yelled. "It's my turn. You've had her long enough."

"Yeah," another boy held his erection in

his hand. "We all get a turn—you promised!"

Paul lurched painfully toward the scene of rape and was once again tripped, this time by a laughing girl. He fell awkwardly, off balance, striking his head on a stone, and was unconscious for a time—how long, he had no way of knowing. When he awakened, strong young hands were holding him to the ground. His mouth was forced open, and straight vodka was poured down his throat. Judy was no longer screaming. Only a grunting sound came from her throat. Some of the young people were staggering about, drunk, laughing and watching the boys taking turns with the rape of Judy.

More vodka was poured down Paul's throat, and then stinging slaps were on his flesh. The older boy was beating him with a belt. Some of the others were whipping his sister with belts. Her cries were pitiful in the night. He saw the older boy's foot draw back, and then there was an explosion in his head. Darkness took him winging away, bright painful lights buzzing in his brain.

After a time, Paul became only vaguely aware of the voices. He did not know where he was, or what was happening. His head throbbed with pain, and there was a huge lump on the side of his head.

"Stupid son of a bitch!" he heard a boy

say. "She's dead! What in the hell are we gonna do?"

"Shut up!" another boy yelled. "Damn you, let me think for a minute, will ya?"

Who is dead? Paul wondered through the pain in his head. He turned his eyes, looking at the boys and girls. They were in various states of undress, and he did not recognize any of them. He seemed to recall someone screaming at some point, but those screams were now silent, only remaining in his mind, echoing about.

"Well, I didn't kill her!" a boy protested. "But we're all in this together—all of us. You all took turns with her. We all hit her with the belt. It's her own damn fault, little cockteaser. You all seen the way she was lookin' at me. She wanted me to fuck her."

"Yeah," a girl said. "It's not your fault. It's her fault, all her fault. We know that."

Her? Paul wondered. *Who are they talking about?*

The radio blared music.

"Turn off that goddamn radio!" a boy said.

Silence in the night.

"What about him?" a boy asked. "He'll tell on us." He began to cry. "I don't wanna go to prison."

"Shut up, sissy face!" the hard voice ordered. "We'll have to do it to him. That's the only way out."

"You mean—?"

"You got any better ideas?"

No one spoke. Only the heavy breathing around the almost dead fire. A few coals glowed dimly. A girl began to weep. The sound of a slap and the command to shut up.

"We'll have to take a blood oath," the hard voice said.

Paul moved his bloody eyes to look at the boy in the dim light from the moon. The boy seemed somehow familiar. An older boy. White flashes of sudden memory blazed through Paul's brain: a girl, held to the ground, that boy between her legs, doing *It* to her. Then there were other flashes: the girl on her knees, with his thing in her mouth. Then the memory faded, leaving Paul with only blackness for a past.

"We'll have to take a blood oath never to tell anyone! We weren't here tonight. We were on the other side of the lake. It's got to be that way. If one tells, we all suffer—go to prison. Maybe get the gas chamber."

They all swore, loud and long, that they would never tell of this night.

Never tell what? Paul wondered.

"We all have to touch them," the older boy said. "Touch their flesh. That way we'll all be a real part of this. That's the only way to make this stick."

One by one, the kids moved to Paul's side, knelt down, and put their hands on him.

They then did the same to Judy. Paul could not move; he seemed paralyzed.

"Who is going to do . . . it?" a girl asked. The voice seemed very far away, as Paul slipped in and out of consciousness.

"You're one of the oldest," a boy said. "And you're the leader of this club. And you were the first to suggest what we did to Judy. And the belt. So I think you ought to be— you know."

"Yeah, that seems fair to me," a voice agreed.

"Yeah."

"Me, too."

As Paul slipped into darkness, he still did not know what was happening around him.

He awakened when he felt the ground grating painfully against his bare skin. He was being dragged over the ground, the rocks and sticks cutting into his naked flesh. And he was cold. The last thing Paul remembered, other than the stars above him, shining brightly, was the sound of water lapping against the shore. It was a peaceful sound in the night as a faraway star winked at him. A friendly wink, so the boy returned the wink. Then a tremendous blow struck him on the head. Pain shot through his body. Another blow, harder than the first, plunged him into shades of gray.

And Paul would remember nothing of this night for years.

Until one day.

One

Denton, Missouri—May, 1999

"Yes." The shaken and stunned father made the identification. "That's my daughter." The sheet was dropped, covering the battered face of young death. The father put his face in his hands and cried, openly and unashamed. "Oh, God!" he cried. "Why her? Why this way?"

You're a great actor, Detective Lieutenant Joe Davis thought, watching the father. *You incestuous son of a bitch.*

The father was gently pulled away from the body and out of the cool, antiseptically clean room in the morgue. Joe waited until he pulled his emotions together.

"Howard, I have to ask you some questions. Sorry, but it's my job. I know it's a bad time."

"All right, Joe. But can't it wait a little longer?"

The two men looked at each other. It was obvious they did not like each other.

The cop nodded. "All right, Howard." He looked at his watch. "I'll come to your house at two this afternoon. Will that be okay?"

Howard Jordan nodded his agreement, reluctantly.

"I'll want to speak with your wife as well."

"She'll be there," he said shortly.

"I'll see you both then."

"Whatever is necessary, Joe."

Only a few miles separated Denton and Red Bay, Missouri, in the heart of the resort and tourist area, and that distance was practically unnoticeable because of the fast food operations, shopping malls, tourist traps (featuring everything from hillbilly music to live rattlesnakes), gas stations, and sub-divisions. The combined population of the two towns was near forty thousand, so the police departments of both towns linked with and became part of the sheriff's department of Morrison County, forming the Red Bay/Denton Sheriff's Department. That move not only gave the citizens more protection, but gave them more professional law enforcement, better trained officers and more equipment.

Detective Lieutenant Joe Davis, a 1975

graduate of Denton High School, had joined the Morrison County Sheriff's Department after serving three years in the army as a member of first the military police, then the army security agency, ASA.

Joe was a bulldog of a cop; once he got his teeth into a case, he was reluctant to turn it loose. His percentage of crimes worked and solved was high above the national average, and the sheriff, T. L. Roberts, considered Joe his best investigator, usually letting him work at his own pace, without interference. Joe would be up for detective captain within the next three years, and few had any doubt that he would make it.

Joe had no interest in running for sheriff; he was too blunt, and had made some enemies. He was a cop, not a politician.

On his desk, in the station house, was a small 5x7 black-and-white photo of a very pretty girl. Her name was Judy Evans, and she had been dead a very long time. Joe remembered the sensational murder well, though he had been a sophomore in high school at the time. He had known Paul and Judy Evans, but not well, and their deaths had saddened him, reenforcing his desire to become a police officer, something Joe had wanted to be since small boy.

The case was still unsolved. And Joe did not like unsolved murder cases. They were so . . . untidy, unprofessional.

For reasons, even he could not name, Joe had never, even as a boy, believed some vagrant had raped, tortured, and then killed the Evans girl—and the boy, although his body was never found. No, even as a boy he believed it had been a person, or persons, living in the Red Bay/Denton community. Further, although he kept his theory private, sharing it with only a very few close and closemouthed friends, he believed that the rich bunch of kids from the Hill Section, that group who had called themselves the Club of the Elite (which had, for some reason, disbanded shortly after the killing of the Evans twins), had something to do with it. And some day, if Joe lived long enough, he would prove his theory.

Over the years, Joe had carefully compiled a dossier on each member of the group. That is how he knew Howard Jordan had incestuous relations with his daughters, Ruth and Donna. He had listened to the rumors, tracked down the source, nailed it shut, and spoken with several nurses at both Red Bay and Denton hospitals. Joe kept those dossiers in a locked desk in his study at home. Occasionally, he studied them, making new notations in his neat script.

Joe knew the lives and the carryings on of the offspring of the Elite Eleven better than any person on earth. Each good man has a fault, and Lieutenant Joe Davis was no exception: he had a dislike—bordering on hatred—for each member of the old Club of the Elite. He disliked them for the taunts he had taken from them as a child from the wrong side of the tracks, their fine new cars (for which they hadn't lifted a finger), new clothes, ski vacations, summers in France, Spain, England, winter vacations in Mexico, Florida—it all came too easily to them. And he disliked them because of who they were. Old reputations in this part of Missouri. Old money. Some wealthier than others, but all very, very comfortable: Jordan, Hartman, Wooten, Rick, Stagg, Harkins, Pike, Lewis, Richard, Kennedy.

They were factory owners, attorneys, landowners, resort owners, highly successful businessmen. And they were snobs. They almost always married within their social group.

Also, Joe knew through hours of legwork, most of their ancestors had made their money through shady, if not downright illegal, business dealings. And the offspring carried on in exactly the same manner.

For all his dislike, Joe never used his position in the sheriff's department to hassle or roust any of them, and he could have very easily done so. He was known throughout the state as an "up and up" cop, unapproachable with any kind of shady deal or bribe, solid and unyielding. He had earned,

twice, the highest medal offered peace officers by the state of Missouri, and the highest
peacetime medal for bravery offered by the
military.

Joe had killed one man while an MP in
the army, and wounded another. He had
killed one man in his fourteen years as a
member of the sheriff's department, and
wounded two. He had broken the arm of
one assailant, the wrist of another, and both
arms of yet another.

Joe Davis had very little compassion for
poor punks. He had risen—pulled himself
up—from almost abject poverty, and believed strongly that anyone else could do
the same, if they had the desire. If they
didn't: to hell with them.

He had absolutely no compassion for rich
punks.

Joe was five-feet, ten-inches tall, and at
first glance appeared to have an average
physique. But on a second, much closer
look, one noticed his huge wrists and fore-
arms. His upper arms were heavily muscled.
Joe boxed in the police gym, practiced
whenever possible on the unarmed combat
range, and was wicked in a stand-up, bare-
knuckle fight. His hair was brown, cut short.
His eyes were blue-friendly or agate mean.
He was a bachelor, forty-one years old.
There was only a touch of gray in his hair.

* * *

Before going to the Jordan house in the Hill Section, Joe went to the county morgue to see if Doctor Williams, the coroner, had returned from Jeff City from a meeting. He had not. He spoke with Doctor Williams' assistant, a young pathologist named Perkins. The pathologist seemed to be flustered about something.

"Uh . . . Joe. I got a confession to make."

Joe allowed one of his rare smiles to crease his face. "What? You gonna tell me you killed the girl?"

"Huh? Hell, no, Joe!"

"Okay, okay, not funny. What confession do you have to make?"

"We . . . I mean, *I* missed something in my preliminary workup on the Jordan girl."

With a cop's patience, Joe waited; Perkins would get to it in time—he hoped.

"I, ah . . . well, I was so flustered, first job without Doc Williams looking over my shoulder, you know, I didn't notice the marks on her back. I mean," he corrected himself, "I *did* notice them, but I thought she probably got them when she was raped. On her back. You know what I mean, Joe, damn!"

Inwardly, Joe came to attention. "What marks?"

"Come on. I want you to see this first-hand."

In the "Stiff Room" (as it was called by the law enforcement personnel of Morrison County, among themselves), Perkins rolled out the locker containing the body of Ruth Jordan. He gently turned the body over on its side, exposing the back and buttocks of the girl. That area was crisscrossed with welts. Perkins was clearly embarrassed by his mistake.

"Uh . . . Joe? You gonna tell Doc Williams that I screwed up on this one?

"No, what's the point in that? I know you won't let it happen again, will you?"

"No, sir."

Joe was on his knees by the body, examining the welts, making notes in his small pad.

The marks had been made, probably, with a heavy leather belt, about two inches wide. "You're sure she was not anally abused."

"Not recently, Joe." Perkins's voice was hard, and full of contempt.

Joe looked up at him. "Yeah, I know," he sighed, getting to his feet. "It happens in the best of families, partner."

"Isn't there anything anyone can do about it, Joe? I mean, you're the lawman."

"It's hard to prove, Charlie. There are centers being set up around the country, but I don't know where the nearest one is around here. And like I said, God, it's tough to prove without all parties coming forth."

Joe walked to the door, tucking away his pad in his hip pocket. He turned around at the door. "You finish with the report on stomach contents yet?"

"Yes, sir. Purple Passion, mostly."

"What?"

"Vodka and grape juice. A lot of it."

"I heard that," Joe said, and walked out the door.

PAUL

Oh, Judy. I'll make them pay. Every one of them. They'll pay for that night so long ago. They'll pay dearly. I'll hunt them for you, and I'll avenge you. As surely as there is a God in heaven and a devil in hell, they'll pay. I'll make them scream out their pain just as you screamed out your pain and humiliation that night. I'll make them pay as you paid, and our parents paid. Our mother, who died of grief; our father, who went insane. I saw him last month, Judy.

I know you did, she answered him. I was with you, remember?

Yes, of course, you were. We saw him, but he did not see us. He put his eyes on us, but did not see us. Poor, pitiful wretch of a man.

Don't dwell on this, Paul.

They'll pay, Judy. Oh, my, yes, how they will pay. I give you my word.

I know, Paul.

On our mother's grave, Judy. By the mental devils that put our father in that awful place. I swear on all those things, Judy. *They will pay.*

I know, Paul. I know.

"Howard, Sissy, tell me, if you can, where Ruth went night before last."

Sissy Jordan began to weep, face in her well-manicured and lotioned hands. Joe waited patiently, his face impassive. He had played this scene many times before.

"She was supposed to have had a date with Dan Hartman," Howard answered. "They were going to one of the senior parties."

"Where?"

"Red Bay."

Joe nodded. "Go on."

"But Dan came down with some kind of stomach bug; his father called and told us. Ruth then said she didn't want to go to the party alone, so she said she'd drive over to Karen Rick's house, to watch TV. I'm tired of telling this story, Joe. My patience is wearing thin over this. Why do we have to keep going over and over it?"

Joe evaded the question. "And that's the last time either of you saw her?"

"Yes."

Sissy began her crying.

"Did Ruth drink much?"

"Certainly not!" Sissy said indignantly, through her tears. "She was only seventeen."

Joe closed his notepad and sighed inaudibly. It was always the same with parents: all the other kids drank and doped, but not their own. *Deaf, dumb, and blind,* Joe thought. *And arrogant, vain, and stupid. Producing perfect children.*

Howard stood up. "I think that will be all, Lieutenant Davis," he announced majestically, as if dismissing a servant.

Which I am, Joe thought, rising from his chair. *A public servant.* "Of course, Mr. Jordan. I think I have all I need."

"When can we . . . get the body?" Howard asked. His wife continued weeping.

Joe looked at Howard and felt the old hate and new contempt rise in him like hot bile. "When Doctor Williams says you can," he answered shortly, much more so than he intended. *You may not like these people,* he reminded himself, *but they have lost a daughter and at least one of them is shocked with grief.* "I know my way out," Joe said, then left.

* * *

"I'm taking you off all other assignments, Joe," the sheriff said back at headquarters. "The Jordan case is yours. Pull as many extra men as you need." He knew Joe would work alone, or at the most, use one or two other men.

"For how long?"

The sheriff met his gaze, then, very unlike him, lowered his eyes. "Until you solve it, Joe. Howard Jordan, Senior, requested you specifically."

"Old Man Jordan hates my guts, T. L., and you know it. This is his way of discrediting me, if I don't break this case."

The sheriff sighed. "Joe, get the chip off your shoulder. You've been carrying it around for too many years. You're the best investigator I've got. You're among the best investigators in this state. Howard Jordan, Senior, does not hate you. Repeat—he does not hate you."

"He killed my father."

"Your father died of a heart attack, Joe."

"And you're conveniently forgetting all the story."

"Just drop it, Joe."

"He was worked to death by Old Man Jordan, then kicked out without a pension or a medical plan, while that fat cat sat on his money bags and purred."

"Times have changed, Joe."

Joe glared at him. "I heard that, T. L."

* * *

Erica Johansen was shocked when Joe approached her desk at headquarters and said, "Give your other cases to someone else, Erica. You're working with me on this Jordan case."

She looked at Joe through pale blue eyes, a wisp of honey blonde hair hanging, as it almost always did, over one eye. She stood up, only two inches shorter than Joe's five-ten. "Would you mind repeating that statement, oh great Morrison County investigator?"

"You heard me," Joe said, then walked into his office.

"Wow!" another detective said, leaning back in his chair. "I don't believe my ears."

"I'll bet," Erica said, "that in the four years I've been with this department the Mighty Joe Davis has not spoken ten words a year to me. He was friendly enough when I first came, and then, boy, did the deep freeze come on."

The third detective on this shift of the day watch leaned back in his chair and smiled up at Erica, his eyes not failing to take in all her highly visible charms. Erica, a beautiful woman of Scandinavian descent, had a lot of charms to be viewed. "If you had but asked, Erica, I would have told you what the problem was."

She looked down at him. "So I'm asking—four years later."

"You went out with Bates Pike when you first got to town. Several times. Joe hates Bates. That dislike goes back to childhood. You'd have to have lived around here to understand."

She sat on the edge of his desk. "So tell me about it."

The detective shook his head. "If Joe wants you to know, Erica, he'll tell you. Right now, you'd better get your tail in his office. As you well know, Joe's all business around the office."

"I never see or hear of him dating anyone, Mike. Does he?"

A slight smile flitted across the cop's face. "Occasionally. Never the same woman more than twice, maybe three times. I think Joe's gun-shy around women."

"Sounds interesting and very elusive. That all you're going to tell me?"

"Ms. Johansen!" Joe's voice blasted through the intercom, with a great deal of emphasis on the *Ms.* "Get a copy of the Jordan file and get in here!"

She grimaced and said, "I think I'll report him to the local chapter of women's lib."

"We don't have one." Mike laughed. "Relax. Joe's bark is worse than his bite. He likes you, Erica."

"Oh? And how do you know that?"

"He told me."

Erica, file folder in hand, knocked on Joe's door, entered at his brusque command, and sat down. "Here I am, Lieutenant Davis. I'm ready."

Joe looked up from his paperwork, a twinkle in his eyes. "Oh?"

This was a side of him Erica had never seen. "To work, lieutenant. To work."

"You can knock off the lieutenant B.S. We're going to be working together on this case—and related cases—for a long time, I'm afraid, so let's make it Joe and Erica, okay?"

She smiled. "That sounds good to me, Joe. What do you mean by 'related cases'?"

"In time, Erica. All in due time." His eyes dropped to the swell of her full breasts then roamed back up to her flawless face. He fished for a cigarette and fumbled for a match, looking in every pocket. He hid smokes and lights in different pockets. Joe had quit smoking eight times in as many years, and was down to less than half a pack a day—with a lot of effort on his part. He met her pale blue eyes. "You know the way I work?"

"Day and night."

"When I'm on a case, sixteen hours a day is not uncommon. Doesn't leave much time for a social life. You object to that?"

"No." She had always been teamed with

other detectives, but never with Joe, and she
looked forward to working with him. Erica
had her degree in criminology, and several
minors in related fields. She had worked
with the KCPD for four years before seeing
and answering an ad in a police publication.
The ad requested applicants to send a re-
sumé to the Red Bay/Denton office. Erica,
tired of city life and its hassles, applied and
was hired. She was twenty-nine.

Joe, on the other hand, had no college
except for a few hours at a local junior college, but he was rated as a good investigator.
A very private man, not known for chitchat,
he was a loner. Self-educated, a voracious
reader of good books, he loved all kinds of
music, from Willie Nelson to Dvorak, and
bass fishing.

Other than that, Erica knew very little
about Joe Davis except she was attracted to
him, and not just in a sexual way. She
wanted to understand him—his moods,
what drove him, what made him tick. And
she fully intended to find out.

Pale blue eyes dropped from off-blue as
the phone rang. Erica listened to the one-
sided conversation with Doctor Williams.

"Sit on the stomach contents of the Jordan girl, Doc," Joe said, and Erica's eyes
widened. "For as long as you can. And when
you put it in the official report, play it down,
if you will, without making a big deal of it."

"Why?" The crusty old man almost shouted the word. Doc Williams wore two hearing aids and had learned to lip-read from necessity.

"You remember the Paul and Judy Evans case, Doc?"

Erica cocked her head to one side and listened, trying to make some sense out of this.

"Of *course* I remember. Hell, Joe, that was twenty-six years ago. You were just a snot-nosed kid at the time, probably beating your donger three times a day and looking for hair to grow in your palm. What's the Evans case got to do with the Jordan girl?"

"The Evans girl was beaten with a belt, marked badly, remember? She had been raped, and her stomach was full of vodka and grape juice."

"Wait a minute, Joe, you're getting ahead of this old man. I got the report from the lab on the Jordan girl right here—some-place. Dammit! Oh, yeah, here it is." The sounds of breathing for a few seconds. "Holy shit!" the old ME said. "The same MO."

"Exactly, Doc. See what I mean?"

"Who have you told about this, Joe?"

"You. And I'm about to tell Erica Johansen. She'll be working with me on this. She'll be the only one working with me."

"If I was ten or fifteen years younger, I'd

like to work with her," the ME chuckled.
"That's a hell of a lot of woman, Joe. She
could wrap those long legs around a man
and put that moss up close . . . my God,
that'd be pure heaven."

Joe laughed at him. "You're a dirty old
man, Doc." He winked at Erica, who could
only guess at what the ME/coroner had
said. She guessed very accurately, but took
no offense. Doc Williams had patted her on
the derrière on more than one occasion,
but he was harmless. She did not know a
soul who did not like the profane old man,
who was a pioneer of modern forensic medi-
cine in Missouri. She had been told Doc
Williams had loudly proclaimed its great-
ness when others in the field of police medi-
cine were calling him a nut. Over the years
he had steadfastly refused to leave Morrison
County, declining much more lucrative of-
fers of work in the city. Doc Williams was in
his late seventies.

"I'll smooth this over, Joe," Williams said,
"but so many years have gone by."

"I know. But I've always had a hunch
about the Evans case. I've discussed it with
you many times."

"Luck to you, boy." He chuckled. "With
the case and with that fine-looking woman.
Hot damn!"

Joe laughed. "I heard that. See ya."

Joe looked at his watch, then at Erica. Hot

damn was right. "It's quitting time. I'll pick you up at your house at seven."

"For what?" She blurted, startled.

"To take you to dinner," he said, smiling.

"Well, of all the nerve! Have you ever thought of asking a lady for permission?"

"No," he replied, then stood up and walked past her, out of his office.

JUDY

It hurt so bad, Paul, she said as he sat in his study. And they did horrible things to me. Ugly things. Things you never knew about.

Tell me.

They did filthy things to me, brother. But that was long ago. Now, you must be careful in what you're doing.

I know. Do you disapprove of what I'm doing?

No. Those responsible must be punished. The law can't, or won't, punish them. So you must.

I will, Judy. I will. For you and for Mother and Father.

And for yourself, Paul. For what they did to you.

Yes. Yes, I will. I promise you.

You're such a good brother, Paul. And I love you.

The man put his face on his desktop and wept.

After her bath, Erica stood naked in front of a full-length mirror and inspected her body. Twenty-nine, and she looked ten years younger. She grinned. Well, five years, at least. Her breasts were full, but youthful in appearance, her stomach firm, legs long and sleek. She was a beautiful woman, and she knew it, but was not vain with the knowledge, just sure of herself.

She glanced at the clock. Six-fifteen. She reached for her gown just as the doorbell rang.

"Oh, damn!" she muttered. "And I'm running late as it is."

"Come on, Erica!" Joe's voice reverberated through the door. "Open up, shake it!"

She threw open the door, anger evident on her face. Her gown, not tightly belted, displayed a large portion of breast.

"Jesus," Joe said, taking a long look.

She flushed, then tightened the belt of her gown. "Now, look, I've had just about enough of your pushy attitude and your bossing me around. You're early, and we've got lots of time—"

Joe cut her off mid-sentence. "Barbara Hartman just ran all out of time." His voice was harsh. "Some kids found her body about ten minutes ago. In a ditch outside of town, on Highway Twenty-two."

"Oh, my God!"

"Can the dramatics, honey. Get dressed in working clothes. I'll wait for you in the car."

Two

"I like you in western clothes," Joe said as they sped to the crime scene, five miles north of Denton. "But I wish you had put on a bra. You're gonna turn on half the sheriff's department with your nipples stickin' out like that. If Carter from MHP is there, he'll be pawin' the ground and snorting like a bull."

She felt a flush creep upward, reddening her face. She was thankful for the darkness of the car. "Are you usually this blunt, Joe?"

"Almost always."

"Well, maybe I dressed like this for your benefit. Ever think of that?"

"If so, thanks." *Great looking tits,* he thought.

"Do you ever get turned on, Joe?" she smiled.

He looked at her for just a moment. "Yeah, Erica, I get turned on."

The police radio squawked its barely intelligible message. Joe acknowledged the call. "On my way."

"Was she. . . ?" Erica asked.

"Beaten and raped."

"Two in less than seventy-two hours."

"There's gonna be a lot more unless we catch this psycho," Joe said. "And catch him fast."

"You seem so certain."

"If this one has the same signs, I *will* be certain. But, oh Lord, I hope I'm wrong."

"What do you mean, Joe?"

"I'll tell you about it—my theory—later. By the way, you like grilled steak?"

His question and shift of subject caught her off guard. "Why . . . certainly."

"Then I'll buy the steaks and salad fixings. We'll fix them at your house. That okay with you?"

"Sure. I'm not afraid to go to your house." She would have liked to see how he lived; a home told a lot about a man.

He smiled, a quick movement of the lips, almost Brando-like.

"I wouldn't want you to think I'm trying to take advantage of you."

"I'm pretty good at judo."

"Ah, trying to intimidate me?"

She put a hand on his thick forearm. "I only went out with Bates Pike a few times. I quickly discovered I didn't like him or his way of life." She felt the muscles in his arm stiffen at the mention of Bates Pike.

"For a fact, Erica, I don't like that

bunch." Then he laughed in the dim light from the dashboard. "I guess it was silly of me, wasn't it? Avoiding you, I mean."

"You're not angry with me for asking questions about you behind your back?"

"No." He grinned boyishly. "Just proves what I've thought all along."

Puzzled, she asked, "And what is that, pray tell?"

"You're lusting after my body."

She punched him on the arm and laughed with him.

Barbara Hartman lay covered with a plastic bag, spotlighted on the cooling earth. A dozen sheriff's department and highway patrol cars were parked close, headlights on, illuminating the ugly and harsh death scene. Erica had slipped a light jacket over her western shirt, smiling at Joe's chuckle as she did so.

"It's cool out," she said.

"I heard that," he replied, using his favorite catchall reply.

Walking to the scene, Joe asked a deputy, "What d'you got?"

"Positive ID on Barbara Hartman. Age seventeen. Looks like she's been dead 'bout twelve hours, give or take a couple."

"Cause of death?"

"Can't be sure. No signs of a struggle here, though."

"Body weight against the ground?"

"Waitin' on you to do that."

"Thanks a lot. Pictures been taken?"

"Just got through."

Joe knelt down and rolled the naked body over to one side. Grass pressings and twig marks on her flesh showed she had been in this spot for some time. The deputy was right, as Joe had suspected he would be: no sign of any struggle at this location.

Without looking up, Joe said, "Cordon off this area—all those woods over there. I don't want anybody in here 'til we can work it clean in the morning."

"Right, Joe."

Erica knelt down beside him and looked at the battered body. "Such a pretty child."

"Was," Joe corrected. "Daughter of one of the Hill Section bunch."

"Like Ruth?"

"Yeah."

Barbara had been severely beaten; she was a mirror image of Ruth Jordan: welts on her back and buttocks, hair matted as if she had been in the water and then allowed her hair to dry without benefit of comb or brush.

"Drowned?" Erica asked.

"I'd bet on it." In the distance, a wail of a siren announced the approach of the ambulance. Joe stood up. "I want this area just as it is in the morning. I don't give a good goddamn how many men it takes, but I don't want anybody stompin' around in here 'til we can work it. Understood?" He spoke to the entire contingent of police officers.

They nodded in unison.

Joe took Erica's arm. "Come on. We'll follow the ambulance in."

"Cause of death?" Joe asked Doc Williams.

"Drowning," the old man replied curtly, as was his fashion. No one who knew him got their feelings hurt. "Just like Ruth Jordan. Everything about them identical."

"Raped?"

"Brutally. We'll have the report on stomach contents in an hour."

"We'll wait," Joe said.

"I never would have guessed," the ME said dryly, then walked down the corridor.

Driving away from the hospital, Erica said, "Everything fits the other, right down to the vodka and grape juice. That's the part I don't understand."

Joe's smile was grim. "I do. And the others will be just the same."

"Others?"

"Oh, there'll be more. Bet on it. What I've feared would happen—has."

She looked at him as he pulled into an all-night supermarket to get the steaks and salad fixings. "And that is?"

His words chilled her, spoken as if they came from a cold grave—which, in effect, they did. "Judy Evans's brother came back."

PAUL

When the boy regained consciousness he was on a slow-moving freight train, in an empty boxcar. He was cold, hurt, and had no recollection of where he was, or who he was. He did not know why he hurt so. It was light out, and the countryside did not look familiar. Pulling some brown paper wrappings from a previous cargo over him, he closed his eyes and slept.

He got off the train in the railroad yard in Joplin. All he wore was his underwear shorts. Animal cunning took over when human intellect left him. Survival was uppermost in his mind.

Clothes and food, he thought. *Then I must go west.*

Why west, he did not know.

In a caboose he found some overalls, shoes, shirt, and a jacket—all too big, but they covered his body and would have to do. He looked in a small mirror. The image looking back at him was unrecognizable: the left side of the face staring at him from the reflecting glass was swollen and bloody. One eye was swelled closed. The head seemed misshapen, ugly, grotesque, something out of a horror story. His upper torso was covered with bruises and cuts, as were his thin arms. He stared at the awful image as long as he dared. Then, when the reflection produced no viable memory, he shrugged his shoulders and turned away, heading out the caboose door.

He ran into a policeman who was searching the empty cars for a jail escapee, violently startling the man. The mangled and bloody boy stunned the cop. The boy ran, and the cop gave chase, but the boy was too swift and the older man gave up after a few hundred yards. He returned to the station house and filed a report on his sighting.

West of Joplin, the boy checked the sun, making certain of his direction, and began trudging west. He walked until noon of that day, until Joplin was far behind him. Then he hopped on a train—heading, he hoped, west.

He was off and on more than a dozen different trains, having been chased by cops and railroad bulls and deputies in a dozen towns and cities along the way. Finally, just east of Denver, he was captured by a brakeman and held until the police arrived. The police took him first to the station house. There, the boy answered all their questions as best he could, while waiting for a doctor to check him.

"But I don't know my name."

"Are you sure, son?"

"Yes, sir. I'm sure."

"Did you run away from home?"

"I don't think so."

"Where is your home?"

"I don't know. I don't think I have one."

"Why did you run away from home?"

"I told you, sir—I don't have a home, and I don't believe I ran away."

"How did you get here?"

"On a train."

"It's not nice to tell lies, son."

"I'm not lying, sir."

Then he was taken to a large hospital. The doctors and the nurses and the staff were kind to him, sympathetic to the young boy with the terrible head wound and no memory. No past. No name.

The doctors agreed on one point: the boy was lucky to be alive.

"You grill a good steak," Erica said. "It was just perfect."

Joe's mind was on the murders and

rapes—and something else. "I've never understood why the parents of Paul and Judy Evans didn't follow up on their murders."

Erica sighed.

"I know they were religious to the point of being fanatic, but I don't understand why they, or how they, could just say it was the Lord's will and then drop it. And I don't understand why the sheriff's department just took it as fact the boy was drowned in Bell Lake. I wonder what deputy worked the case?"

"Did they drag the lake?" Erica had accepted the fact they were going to talk about murders until she could tactfully change the subject—if that were possible, which she doubted.

"Yeah, and all the little creeks that ran in and out of it—so I'm told. But some of those creeks are swollen in the spring, and more than one flows into the maze of lakes around here."

"And your conclusion is . . . ?"

"Paul's alive. And he's here in this area, killing the kids of the people who raped and killed his sister."

"Then let's prove it," Erica said.

"It's not gonna be easy, and until we produce some hard evidence we're gonna have to keep our mouths shut about what we're doing."

"I think that would be best."

"It's gonna be a seven day a week job," he warned her.

"All right."

"I'm a slave driver."

She laughed. "Other words for male chauvinist pig, you mean."

"Believe me, I've been called worse." He grinned, then leaned over and kissed her on the lips. Before she could respond to his kiss—which she desperately longed to do— he was on his feet and moving toward the door. "I'll be honking for you at eight o'clock in the morning."

"But tomorrow's Saturday! Can't we make it ten o'clock?"

"Just think of all the overtime you're going to collect." Then he was gone, the door slammed closed behind him.

Erica stamped her foot. "Damn!" she said. Then she looked around, a smile forming on her lips. "Well, he's no fool. He got out before I could ask him to help with the dishes."

"If I do this . . . thing," Barbara Hartman had asked, a whining tone to her voice. "Will you let me go?"

"Yes." The man smiled at her. "Of course. You have my word." He cupped her young breasts, squeezing. He squeezed harder, and she cried out in pain.

"I thought you were a nice man!" she wailed.

"I am." He laughed insanely. "And I'm going to be nice to you." He held his hardness close to her face as he pushed her to her knees. "And if you bite me, I promise you this—I'll torture you for days, until you beg me to let you die."

"I'll be good to you!" she cried. "Just don't hurt me any more." And she leaned forward and took him.

"Nothing!" Joe said disgustedly. He wiped sweat from his face. "Not one damn shred of evidence we could use."

Erica sat down on a log near the edge of the woods where Barbara's body was found. "This guy knows what he's doing. He's nobody's fool."

"He's smart. I'll give him that much. Smart, but warped."

"Why don't we go to Sheriff Roberts and put all the cards on the table about your theory? Tell him what you suspect."

"It's too soon. He knows I hate those people. He wouldn't believe me. Remember this: those are money-people—powerful people in this state. We're going to have to have some hard evidence to show him, and that we don't have. Not yet."

"Reading between the lines, what you're saying is someone else has to die?"

He sighed heavily and nodded his head. "That's it, I'm afraid."

That's a rocky road to travel." She looked up at him.

"I know, but I don't think the road is very long. He's going to strike again, very soon. When we get back to headquarters, we'll start a file of the Eleven and their kids, make it as comprehensive as possible. I want to talk with some retired cops around here again, and firm up my files as to just who was in that old club they had. I think I know most of them, but I want to be sure.

"Howard Jordan has a twisted streak in him, Erica. I know that for a hard fact. He was cruel as a boy, liked to hurt things, living things. You won't find any official record of this, but Howard was hauled in several times for roughing up dates. If his old man hadn't had money, lots of money, Howard would have been sent to the bucket as a young man—for rape. I know of at least three times his father had to buy Howard out of charges. At the very least, he would have been sent to the state hospital for psychiatric treatment.

"I know Judy and Paul Evans were asked to join that kids' club Howard formed. And I can prove that. The cops questioned all members after Judy's death. But the families who make up the old Elite Eleven had too much money and too much power for the cops to push their investigation. It's sad, but that's the way things were back then, and still are, to some degree. Howard Jordan, Junior, killed Judy Evans. I know it, and I've known it for years. But I just can't prove it. Not yet."

She rose from the log to face him, her breasts only a few inches from his chest. "This is all so sad, Joe. Graduation should be a time of fun for the kids. Parties, and all that."

"Well, I'll tell you this, Erica—for many of them, it's going to be a time to die."

The time to die came to Joy Grotin Pike, wife of Henry Pike, and mother of June, a junior at Denton High. Joy's first mistake was in joining the Club of the Elite, back in '73. Her second mistake was in marrying Henry Pike. Her third was driving her daughter's car to the shopping mall on Saturday morning. And her fourth mistake was in stopping to chat with a friend.

Joy Grotin Pike vanished.

"All right," Joe said, looking at the large posterboard thumbtacked to a wall of his study at home. "There it is. The genealogical breakdown of the Elite Eleven. The fourth and fifth generations, that is. Mothers, fathers, and kids—forty-seven potential victims—minus two. But it's too soon to find a pattern to work from."

Beside him, Erica shivered.

"Cold?" Joe asked.

"No," she said. She wondered if she could ever adopt the cop's lack of emotion when speaking of the dead, or soon-to-be-dead.

"So what did you discover this afternoon?"

"I spoke with Lou and Ginny Pappas. Ginny was originally a Green. Not quite a member of the Hill Section society; her parents were comfortable, but not comfortable enough to be a part of that group."

"I know her. Class of seventy-four. I don't know Lou very well."

"He came here from St. Louis in nineteen seventy-nine. Took over the old Eaton Hills Hotel and made a go of it. Married Ginny in nineteen eighty-one."

"Yeah. Kind of a scandal about her marrying what her friends called a foreigner. But from what I hear about Lou, he's a nice guy."

"He is. The flap was about religion. Lou's Catholic, Ginny's Baptist. This is big Baptist country, and never the faiths shall mix, and all that crap."

"Anyway, neither of them care for Howard Jordan. Seems that Ginny dated Howard once. Just once."

"Yeah. That happened while I was in the army. But I heard about it when I got back. I told you about Howard."

"It wasn't rape, but it was awfully close. That cost Howard's father a bundle. Both Lou and Ginny told me quite a bit about Howard and his, ah, extracurricular activities."

"That are still going on."

"Oh, my, yes. Joe, they told me Howard, they thought, is having incestuous relations with both of his daughters."

"He is, and with anyone else's daughter or wife he can get his hands on. Howard is a lowlife bastard but big money has kept him out of the slammer for years."

"Anyway, Ginny was invited to join that Club of the Elite back in high school. She went to one meeting, didn't like what she saw, and left. Never attended another."

"And. . . ?" Joe prodded patiently.

"Ginny says the Evans twins were invited to a meeting of that club. They talked about it at school. The very next weekend, they disappeared."

"That was twenty-six years ago this June. The twins were thirteen, according to school records, those that I could find, that is. That would make Paul thirty-nine."

"If he's alive."

"He's alive," Joe said, certainty in his voice. "And he's here."

"You!" Joy gasped through her pain and tears. "All these years it was you!"

"Did you enjoy seeing my sister suffer that night, Mrs. Pike?" The man **gri**nned down at her. "Did you enjoy listening to her cries for help?"

"We were all drunk!" Joy screamed. The floor was cold against her nakedness. Her flesh ached from the beating she had received. "Drunk! What happened was an accident. You've got to believe me. Please! For the love of God."

"Liar!" he screamed, swinging the heavy belt, laughing as the studded leather smashed her flesh, again and again.

Joy Grotin Pike huddled on the dirty floor, crying.

He left her for a moment, her face pressed against the floor. She was praying.

She looked up from her bruising beating. She screamed at the sight of him, naked above her.

"No!" she wailed. "Oh, my God—*nooo!*"

"Maybe it's not the same man," Erica said, nauseated at the sight of Joy Grotin Pike on the table.

"The MO is the same," Joe said. "Yeah, it's the same dude." *Just wanted a mother to experience the pain of virgin rape,* he thought.

"This guy is one heavy hung dude," Charlie Perkins observed.

"What a marvelous expression," Erica noted.

Doc Williams snorted. "We've got a real pervert on our hands, people. There is no evidence of semen, so I can only assume the rapist used a dildo, of mammoth proportions."

"Either that, or she was raped by a great ape," Charlie said.

"I can do without your feeble attempts at humor, young man," Doc Williams glared at him.

Screwed her to death, Joe thought. "Cause of death?"

"Same as the others," the ME said. "But she would have bled to death, anyway. The damage was extensive."

"But why a dildo on her and not on the others?" Charlie asked.

Joe and Erica exchanged glances with Doc Williams. The three offered no answer to Charlie's question, but all felt they knew why.

"How many times was she assaulted?" Erica asked.

"My dear," Williams grimaced, "there is no way I can answer that. But taking into consideration the condition of her body, I would have to say many, many times."

"Perhaps," Perkins conjectured, attempting to regain Doc Williams's favor, "the rapist is compensating for his lack of ability and bulk by using a dildo?"

"Perhaps." Williams was noncommittal. Again, he exchanged glances with Joe and Erica.

"How close are we to capture of this nut?" the voice came from behind them. Sheriff Roberts.

"I think we're getting closer," Joe said.

"How close?" the sheriff demanded.

"Not close enough," Joe admitted.

"Three rape murders in less than four days." Roberts shook his head. "The same MO in all of them. The national press is gonna be crawling all over us in a few days if this keeps up. I'm under pressure, Joe— from the bigwigs in this town—so I'm setting up a task force."

"All they'll do is muddy the waters, T. L.," Joe said. "Give Erica and me a few more days on this."

"Hear me out. I was about to say that you and Detective Johansen work separately from the task force. Let them do the leg work. You two stay with your snooping. It's this way or nothing. I've got heat on me." He looked worried.

Joe nodded. "How's Henry taking this?"

"Rough. He's outside now, with Reverend Banning. Henry wants to see his wife again."

"I would strongly advise against that," Doc Williams said. "He went to pieces making the ID."

"It's his wife, Doc," Roberts said. Then he plopped his cowboy hat on his head and left.

"You know," Perkins said, "this rapist is no dummy. With tourist season just getting under way, this area is full of strangers. You think he planned it that way?"

I think he's been planning this for years, Joe thought. *Waiting for the girls to grow up.* "I don't know," he replied. "Maybe. Who knows the mind of a psycho?"

Henry Pike walked unsteadily into the room, helped along by his minister, Reverend Phil Banning. A tall, heavily muscled man, Reverend Banning attempted to tend to the needs of his jaded flock, many of whom were from the Hill Section.

Henry seemed almost unaware of the police and the doctors, his eyes fixed on the now sheet-covered coolness of his wife. "Let me see her," he whispered.

"Henry, please," Reverend Banning said.

"Wait 'til later, Henry," Doc Williams urged.

He was waved away by the grieving husband. "I want to see her, Doc."

Williams shrugged, then drew back the sheet, exposing the face of Joy Grotin Pike. Any farther and the husband would have seen the crisscrossings of autopsy.

Henry looked at her battered face, then fainted, falling almost soundlessly to the tile floor.

While Henry was being attended to in the emergency room of the hospital, Joe and Erica talked in a reception area with Reverend Banning, Father Cary, the Catholic priest, and a woman Joe detested—Debbie Harkins, a close friend of Joy Pike. She left the group to see to Henry (it was common knowledge she was having an affair with him, as well as with Howard Jordan), and Joe was glad to see her go.

"I've advised all my people to keep a close watch on their children," Phil Banning said. "And to please cease all these graduation parties immediately. Father Cary has done the same."

"And. . . ?" Erica asked.

"I don't believe we succeeded," Father Cary replied in his soft voice. He glanced at Phil. "We have spoken with Dick Ballard of the Baptist church, and he concurs, of course, as do all the other ministers we've contacted." He sighed. "But kids being kids, and all that . . ." He shrugged.

"So the parties will continue?" Joe questioned bitterly.

"I believe they shall," Phil said. "We can only advise, Lieutenant Davis, not command."

"Joe." Erica touched his arm. "I wonder if the city fathers of Denton and Red Bay would consider a curfew?"

"Excellent suggestion," Phil said, and the priest nodded his head in agreement.

"Not unless the situation worsens," Doc Williams said, walking up to join the group. "I don't have to tell you—any of you—about today's parents or their offspring. Parents today are wishy-washy, and the kids would rebel at a curfew—especially these spoiled brats in this area."

"And sneak around and have their parties in secret." Erica agreed with the ME.

"Yeah," Joe said. "I think our best bet—short of any curfew—is to talk with the parents. For whatever good that will do."

Doc Williams snorted derisively. "If today's parents had an ounce of gumption in them, we wouldn't have the dope and moral problems we all have to cope with. When I was a boy we could buy all sorts of powerful drugs, some of them right across the counter at any apothecary shop. But we didn't. Wanna know why? Because our fathers would have kicked the shit out of us, that's why! You would all be amazed at what wonders a good smack across the mouth can bring. You people, these communities, have a large problem with this nut running around. But don't expect much help from the parents—they're afraid of their own children. I wish you all a lot of luck." He stalked down the glaringly lighted corridor.

"Not a very optimistic man," Phil opined, his eyes on the doctor's retreating back.

"I guess he's seen a lot of tragedy in his time," Erica mused. "A lot of useless deaths."

"And he's gonna see a lot more before we catch this screwball that's running around," Joe said.

Neither saw the look in Father Cary's eyes.

PAUL

I can detect a tremble of fear beginning to race through the community, Judy. But I don't believe those responsible for your death have put it all together yet. I don't believe they realize I've returned.

Be careful, Paul. Don't get caught before you complete what you returned to do.

I won't.

* * *

Sunday passed quietly, much to everyone's relief, especially those in the law enforcement field. Doc Williams released the bodies of Ruth Jordan and Barbara Hartman for burial. It was a double funeral. The funeral of Joy Grotin Pike would be held Tuesday.

Monday afternoon, just after the funerals, a small package arrived at the home of Howard and Sissy Jordan.

Sissy's screaming brought her husband on the run. He had not yet returned to his office, and their only surviving child was at the home of a friend.

His wife was alternating between incoherent babbling and wild screaming. She stood pointing at the box.

Inside was a newspaper picture of Judy Evans.

Three

Seven o'clock. Monday evening.

"Joe!" Erica's voice rang in his ear when he stilled the ringing of the phone. "Big doings at the Jordan house. Must be a dozen cars parked there."

"Senior party?"

"No. All the kids are at a heavily guarded dance tonight, at the Stagg home on the lake."

"Can you pick me up in ten minutes?"

"On my way."

She picked him up in her Nissan 200SX, equipped with a police band radio and CB. "I was restless after I got off work," she said, rolling away from the curb, "so I decided to take a drive. I drove east, past the Hill Section, and I noticed all those cars pulling in. I parked down the road, in the parking area of that closed-down little grocery, and started counting cars. They're all there, Joe.

Every member of the old Club of the Elite. All except Henry Pike."

"Something's popping." He stuck a cigarette between his lips and began his searching for a light. "Maybe they've finally made the connection?"

"Something else, and I don't know if it's connected."

He looked at her. The cigarette dangled between his lips; he had left his matches at home, in his other jacket.

"Father Cary's been driving past, up and down, back and forth. Kind of aimlessly."

"That is odd." Joe was silent for a time, noticing she handled the sports car skillfully, smoothly. "Paul Evans was a small boy," he said, almost to himself. "Had some sort of ailment as a child. Rheumatic fever, I think it was. May have stunted his growth."

"Father Cary is a small man."

"I heard that. You got any matches on you?"

"No. And I jimmied the lighter so it won't work."

"Thanks a bunch," he muttered, sticking the cigarette back in his pocket. "Paul would be about thirty-nine now. We'll run a make on Father Cary after we check out the Jordan house."

"I called DMV just before I called you. Father Cary *is* thirty-nine."

"Well, now." Joe smiled. "I'll make a detective out of you yet."

She smiled, thinking: *I'd be happy if you just made me.* Then she blushed at her erotic thoughts. She said, "Let's run a check on everybody that's moved into this area during the past five years—if we can, that is."

He whistled. "Big job. But we can give it a whirl."

She was suddenly depressed. "But we don't even know if Paul, or whatever name he's using, even lives around here. Maybe he just blew in."

"We have to start somewhere, babe."

Babe? Her depression vanished.

"I can think of a half-dozen suspects right off the bat," Joe said. "That's what I was doing when you called. Putting some names on paper. David Hicks, the new English teacher at Red Bay. Gene Taylor, the mechanic at the Olds place. He's been in trouble before. James Smith, the insurance agent at Wallace Insurance. Hal Risten over at Neal's Bar. Martin Sterling, the assistant manager at Patton's Department Store. Chris Northcutt, that weird ass artist who lives up in the hills just north of town." He grimaced. "If what he paints can be called art."

She laughed at him. "It's modern art."

"It stinks," was his reply. "I wouldn't hang that crap in an outhouse."

She shook her head, grinning. "So we've got a big job ahead of us."

"I heard that. Here we are. Damn! Look at the cars. The clan has indeed gathered."

"I'd love to go in there."

"That's exactly what we're going to do."

"You're kidding. We just can't barge in a private home."

He smiled. "You just watch and follow my lead."

"Evening, Mr. Jordan," Joe said as the front door was pulled open.

"Uh, what are you. . . ." He noticed Erica, his eyes traveling up and down her body. She felt as though she were being undressed by his eyes. She was. ". . . . and your friend doing here?"

"We saw someone run around the cars parked out front. Looked like he was carrying something. Hubcaps, maybe. Thought we'd check it out. That is, if you want us to."

"Ah . . . why certainly, Joe. All sorts of thieves running around these days."

"We'll give you a report as soon as we're finished. Shouldn't take long."

"Fine." He shut the door in their faces.

Walking through the curving drive, among the many parked cars, Erica said, "He looked flustered. Upset."

"I noticed. Was it my imagination, or did I hear someone crying in the house?"

"I heard it. A woman. I don't like that man."

His laugh was bitter and short, a human bark in the night. "Join the club. Howard's a prick!"

"Why do you dislike him so?"

"He's arrogant, and he didn't work for what he has. That's two of many reasons."

"Tell me the rest of the reasons sometime?"

"Sure."

The pair walked the grounds, flashlights in their hands, then once again knocked on the door of the mansion.

Howard's face was flushed. Whether from anger, excitement, or fear, the cops did not know, but he was upset.

"It's all clear, Mr. Jordan," Joe said. "I can't find anything missing from the cars. Sorry to have bothered you tonight."

"That's quite all right. I'm just glad our sheriff's department is so observant. Good night." He shut the door in their faces.

"Arrogant ass!" Erica said, driving down the long blacktop drive and onto the street.

"Among other things," Joe said.

* * *

1

"Is he on to us?" Debbie Harkins asked. Her husband, Peter, had his head practically stuck in a brandy bottle, well on his way to becoming plastered and eventually passing out, as was his habit every evening.

"I don't know," Howard replied. "But I do know he'd just love to hang us with something. Father should have had him run out of town years ago."

"Be that as it may," Vic Woten observed, "we certainly can't go to the police with any of our suspicions. We've got to handle this ourselves, and do it quietly. And quickly. The question is, how?"

"I just can't believe that Paul is still alive," Linda Lewis said as she gnawed at her fingernails. She glared at Howard. "You said you killed him that night. We took a blood oath, and you said you killed him!"

"Goddamn you!" Howard raged at her. "You all saw me hit him with that club. He can't be alive! I bashed his head in and threw him in an empty boxcar. The whole side of his head was caved in. I couldn't find a pulse, a heartbeat, breathing—nothing! He was dead." He poured a snifter of brandy, drank it, and calmed himself. "No, this isn't Paul. This is someone who merely suspects. A cheap blackmail plan, I'll wager.

Might even be Joe Davis. It would be like him. He hates us all."

"What do we do, Howard?" Louise Rick asked.

"Nothing. Keep calm. Don't get hysterical like my wife did this afternoon."

Debbie's eyes were hot on him as she asked, "How is Sissy?"

"Asleep. I gave her a large sedative. She'll be all right, I assure you." He glanced at Peter, who was nodding off in an easy chair. For a quick second, Debbie caught Howard's eyes, smiling. He said, "Just stay calm and go about your business. If anything else occurs . . . well, we'll just have to play it by ear. Right now, let's break up this meeting before that snoopy little janitor's son returns."

The remaining sons and daughters and spouses of the Elite Eleven filed out. No one said anything about Peter asleep in the chair, passed out, or that Debbie was staying. Most had their little affairs, and everyone in the group knew who was sleeping with whom.

Peter snored drunkenly in his chair, a bit of spittle oozing from the corner of his mouth. Debbie rose as the last car pulled away from the mansion. She walked to Howard, slipping her arms around him, pressing against him.

"You're sure it's safe?" she questioned. "No chance of Sissy waking up?"

Howard grinned down at her, touching his mouth to hers. "Not a chance. I gave her a pill large enough to fell an ox." He cupped her buttocks with his hands and squeezed.

She ground her pelvis against him, running her tongue over his lips. "Peter was half-looped before we came over here. Had several martinis. I counted six double brandies here. He'll be out for at least a few hours."

They moved to a small bedroom off the study. She stripped, jerking off her panty hose, ripping them in her haste. She lay on the bed, spreading her legs, her fingers busy. "Hurry up, Howie, I'm dripping all over the sheet."

Howard crawled between her legs and took her with one long thrust, bringing a grunt of pain and pleasure pushing past her lips.

They coupled like animals in heat, her legs wrapping about his, both of them mumbling absurdities mixed with vulgarities. So busy in satisfying their lusts, they did not notice Sissy as she slowly made her way down the winding steps from the master bedroom on the second floor of the mansion. She saw Peter passed out in the chair, then followed her ears to the grunting from the off-study bedroom. She walked to the side of the open bedroom door and stood there for a time, listening, a grimace of distaste and disgust parting her lips.

Ruth still warm in her grave, she thought, *and all my husband can think of is Debbie's cunt.* She shook her head. She had known for some time that her husband was having sexual relations with their daughters, but she didn't know what to do about it. Surely, she could not go to the police. That would bring disgrace upon them. She touched the small of her back, feeling the bruise through her nightgown where Howard had beaten her—again. He occasionally beat her, forcing her into perverted acts. Howard liked to inflict pain on women. And he was not above rape.

The thought came to her: could Howard be the murderer?

She pushed that thought from her mind as quickly as it came. Then she listened for a time longer, revulsion growing in her.

The couple shifted positions on the bed, Debbie on her knees, Howard behind her, servicing her.

Sissy turned away before it became perverted, as she knew it could, for she knew her husband well, knew all his perversions.

"Oh, Christ!" Debbie cried out. "That hurts, Howie!"

"Want me to stop?" He panted the question.

"No! A little more!"

Sissy walked back up the elegant steps to the master bedroom, thinking: *At least he'll leave me alone tonight.*

2

Tuesday, Wednesday, and Thursday passed without murder or rape in the Red Bay/Denton area. Joy Pike was buried and Henry and his only child, June, attempted to put some order back in their lives.

Friday afternoon Joe and Erica were immersed in paperwork: reports of a hundred or more men who had moved into the Red Bay/Denton area over the past few years. Erica worked alongside Joe in his small office, and neither of them noticed when the door opened. Sheriff Roberts finally cleared his throat to get their attention.

"T. L." Joe looked up, acknowledging his boss's presence and taking in the worried look in the sheriff's eyes.

"Getting anywhere?" Roberts asked grimly. "Either of you?"

"We've eliminated a lot of people," Joe replied. "If that's getting anywhere."

Erica smiled at him. "Plus, we've had a few days without trouble."

Roberts sighed. "Well, that time of peacefulness just ended. Kit Lewis and Yvette Mack have just been reported missing. Our boy is out prowling."

Joe snapped a pencil in half and Erica closed her eyes, both of them waiting for the other to ask the question.

Joe asked. "How long have they been missing?"

"Since ten o'clock this morning."

A detective stuck his head into the office. "Joe? That mechanic at the Olds place, Gene Taylor? He's been missing all day. I just talked with the shop foreman. He didn't report for work this morning, and no one answers at his apartment."

"Pick him up for questioning," the sheriff said. "Easy, now, we don't want to violate his goddamn constitutional rights."

The phone rang. It was for the sheriff. Roberts listened for a few seconds, his face paling with each tick of the clock in the squad room. He gently replaced the phone in its cradle.

"A fisherman just reported spotting two bodies floating in Bell Lake. Said it looked like two girls. He called the local game warden."

Joe and Erica were running for the car before the words left the sheriff's mouth.

* * *

3

"I've never seen anything like this," the young game warden said. He looked as though he might throw up any minute. "God! They're so young!" He walked away, behind a clump of bushes. The sounds of his vomiting drifted out.

Kit and Yvette lay under a tarp. Both had been tortured, raped, and murdered. Their bodies were horribly mutilated.

"A new twist has been added." Erica paled at the sight. "I wonder if they were alive when . . . this was done to them?"

"Five'll get you ten they were," Joe replied. "And their stomachs will be full of vodka and grape juice." He pulled a much-folded and creased piece of paper from his jacket pocket, a short report on Paul Evans he had put together. "Remember what Paul Evans collected as a boy?"

"Knives and swords," she said. "The report said he was fascinated with cutlery."

"And when the detectives entered Gene Taylor's apartment a short time ago . . . ?"

"They found over a dozen hunting knives, and many more pocket knives. Think this Taylor is our boy?"

"I don't know, Erica. It all seems too easy to suit me. Too pat."

"That's the feeling I get."

"Get it squared away here," Joe ordered

his men. "All time off is cancelled. Sheriff Roberts says we're all working twelve hour shifts, effective immediately."

PAUL

You're a fool, Paul! Now, they'll know it's you! Why did you use the knife?

Paul hung his head, listening to his sister's voice scold him. I had to, he said. I wanted to hear them scream as you did that night. They're all twits—just like their parents. They deserve to die.

I did not mean to rage at you, Paul, her voice came to him. But you must be more careful after this.

Yes, I will.

Just hours before the boy was to be turned over to the juvenile authorities in Colorado, he ran away, heading west. At poolside in Las Vegas, he stole the wallet of a young man, filled with money and ID, and continued on his westward journey.

He had spent almost nine months in the hospital in Denver, undergoing several operations, including surgery to repair his battered and ruined face. The good food, constant care, and regular exercise had filled him up and out. He looked older than his fourteen years.

The Denver Police had fingerprinted him, but the young man had never been fingerprinted before; there was no record on file, anywhere.

He bummed up and down the west coast, mostly California, for two years, but always returned to the Sacramento area, where he was nearly caught a dozen times. He changed identities ten times in three years. Then, in 1978, he broke into a high school in Fresno, built himself a transcript and a diploma, assumed a name he had taken from a driver's license years before in Las Vegas, and joined the Air Force. There, he picked up a few hours of college. Upon discharge, he went to college on his GI bill, and graduated with honors.

He still had no memory of his past.

4

"You got no right to treat me thisaway!" the mechanic protested. "I ain't done nothing."

"You have been advised of your rights, Mr. Taylor," Erica told him. "Has anyone mistreated you in any way?"

He shook his head. "No, I guess not. But

I still ain't done nothing for you to bring me here."

"I'll ask you again, Mr. Taylor," Joe said, the cassette recorder running. "Do you wish to have an attorney present during this questioning?"

"I don't know no lawyer."

"Would you like for us to get you an attorney?"

Again, he shook his head. "I guess not. What is it you want from me?"

"Where were you today, between nine this morning and two this afternoon?" The time of death for Kit and Yvette had been tentatively established at between eleven and two.

"Oh, man!" the mechanic jerked his head up. "I know what this is about. Hey, I never raped no one in my life, and I damn sure never killed no one."

"Then tell us where you were between those times," Joe urged.

"Man, you don't know what you're asking! That woman'll kill me—if her husband don't do it first."

"What woman?" Erica asked.

"The woman I was with."

"Who is she?"

Taylor sighed. "Look, people, I just can't say. Her old man is a big shot in this area. Look," he pleaded, "I got a good job, make good money. But he'll run me slap outta this county. I'll tell you what. I'll take a lie detector test and prove you wrong. 'Cause I ain't done nothing!"

"Have you been been in trouble with the law before coming here?" Joe asked.

"Sure," the man replied. "I been in jail for drinkin' and fightin' some, down south in Georgia. And I had a speeding ticket, 'bout three years ago. And that's all."

Joe and Erica knew he was telling the truth. Gene Taylor had been run through the National Crime Information Center's computers, and he was clean. No wants, no warrants, no serious priors.

"You like knives, Mr. Taylor?" Erica asked.

His face brightened. "I sure do! My daddy used to make 'em down in Georgia. I've got a house full of 'em. Why, I can take a spring off a car and make you the finest knife you ever owned. I'll be glad to do it for you, anytime."

"You want that polygraph test now, Mr. Taylor?" Joe asked.

"I sure do."

He was given both a polygraph and PSE (psychological stress evaluator). Both operators said he was telling the truth: Gene Taylor had been with a married woman that morning, at a motel just outside of Denton. He had killed no one, raped no one.

Back in Joe's office, Taylor finally told the cops the name of the woman he'd been with. Both Erica and Joe smiled. They both knew the woman, and her reputation. Besides, Taylor had firm alibis as to his whereabouts when the other girls had been raped and killed. He was released, asked not to leave town. His file would remain open.

A detective walked into the office. "Joe, we may have a little something here. KCPD reports that Dave Hicks, that English teacher at Red Bay High School, was under investigation for rape when he was in high school, back in seventy-three. There was also a series of rapes and near-rapes on the campus of U of M when he was a student in seventy-five and seventy-six. Unsolved."

"Where was he today?"

"The principal said he called in sick this morning, but came to work this afternoon and held his classes."

"Check him out."

"There's more. We got two possibles here in this community, in addition to Hicks and Taylor. Willie Winston's got a 'jacket' on him an inch thick, everything from contributing to the delinquency of a minor to assault with a deadly weapon. He was a pimp in St. Louis, used to like to beat up his whores. But he's been Mister Goody Two-Shoes for as long as he's been around here. Not a ripple on him. And Chris Northcutt, that weird artist lives up in the hills? Guess where he learned to paint?"

"I'm all ears, Mike."

"The state pen." The detective smiled. "Where he was doing time for rape."

5

"You said you'd tell me why you dislike those people so," Erica prompted Joe. Dinner at his house was good: huge salad, spaghetti, garlic bread, and wine. "Anything wrong with now, or don't you trust me?"

They ate in silence for a couple of minutes. She could tell he was collecting his thoughts, making up his mind.

They finished the meal, stacked the dishes in the dishwasher, and he poured them another glass of wine. "Let's sit in the den," he suggested.

The night was cool, so Joe built a small fire in the fireplace. He stood for a time, looking into the flames. "My father was illiterate, and my mother was a drunk," he said. The words came painfully.

Erica sighed, almost knowing what was coming next.

"Dad worked at odd jobs most of his life. When I was a kid, the year Mother died, he got a job as a janitor with Jordan Enterprises. I went to school here, in Denton." He sighed. "I would have preferred to have gone to Red Bay, away from those snobby kids. But . . ." He shrugged.

"I'm not unique, Erica. My story is played out in every city and town and village in America, every day—it always will be. I shouldn't dislike the Elite kids—they are only what their parents made them—but I can't help it. They gave me a pretty rough time of it."

"Kids can be so cruel," she murmured.

"Yes, they can. Believe me, I know."

"Joe, you're leaving something out."

He turned from the flames to look at her. "You're pretty sharp, aren't you?"

She said nothing, just met his eyes with hers.

"I had a sister," he said, after a moment's pause.

"And . . . ?"

"Let's just say she turned out—kind of bad."

"Had a sister?"

"She's dead."

"I'm sorry. That's such an inadequate phrase, isn't it? Was she younger or older?"

"Older, by several years."

Erica sat on the couch and watched him struggle for words to tell his story in his own way.

"Madge, that was her name, had a wild streak in her. I won't try to cover that up. She was pretty, and knew it. Pretty and poor. She and Howard were the same age, same class in school. He said Madge led him on, teased him into doing . . . what happened. But I didn't believe it then, and I don't believe it now. They were both only thirteen."

"Oh, Joe—"

He ignored her, plunging into the story. He seemed relieved, after all these years, to have someone listen, to get it off his mind. "You see"—the words were tinged with bitterness—"that's how Dad got his job at Jordan Enterprises. Dad agreed not to press charges in exchange for a lifetime job at Jordan Enterprises. No pension plan, no health insurance. Hell, Dad couldn't read or write much. He didn't know what he was putting his mark on. He was waiving all fringe benefits. This was years ago, Erica."

She shook her head in disgust.

"Dad was in his mid-fifties when he had his first heart attack. On the job. He always worked the late shift. But only the doctor knew about it, and Dad made him promise not to tell any of us. He kept right on working. He died at work a year later."

"Where was Madge?"

"Oh, I finally located her in St. Louis. She'd been a prostitute for years. On her own, that is."

"On her own? I don't understand, Joe."

"Howard kept her in the city for a few years. Furnished her an apartment, kept her in clothes, the whole bit. All she had to do was entertain him and his college friends, when they came to the city." He laughed acidly. "Howard is twisted, Erica, bent all out of shape sexually. Name something perverted, and Little Howie likes it. Madge told me once, when she was still speaking to her baby brother, that Howard used to bring several guys at a time to see her. Howard liked to watch while she entertained them."

"That's disgusting!" she spat out the words, as if their sound left a bitterness on her tongue. "But why didn't she leave him? Just get out?"

Joe's eyes were sad and angry. "Same old story, babe. Howard got her hooked on drugs. He'd supply her just enough to keep her going, but not enough to destroy her looks—for a time. Oh, yeah, Madge was quite a swinger for a time, thanks to Little Howie and his friends, some of whom still live in this community. The goddamn snooty perverted bastards!"

She knew from station talk that Joe had quite a temper when angered, and that he was like a mad bull in a fight. "From what I heard concerning your temper," she said, "I'm surprised you never beat up Howard."

He grinned a small smile. "Oh, I braced him a couple of times after I got out of the army. Once in St. Louis, once in Kansas City. But he wouldn't fight. On top of everything else, Howard is a coward."

"How did your sister die?"

Once again, a sigh. "She kept going downhill, little by little, drifting from pimp to pimp, getting the shit beat out of her to try to keep her in line, to dampen her spirit—which was impossible. She began to suffer from mental illness—I don't know what kind of mental illness. She was institutionalized several times. One night she ran off from the mental hospital, went back to St. Louis, and took a header off a bridge, into the Mississippi. Her body was never found. End of Madge."

"How long ago was that?"

"Years."

She sensed he did not want to talk of it further; he had said all he was going to say of the past.

Their eyes met, locked, held, as a spark began moving between them, shuttling back and forth, touching the man and woman intimately. Erica rose from the couch and walked to the man standing by the small fire.

The heat in the room did not come only from the flames.

She smiled at him, this woman, all woman, her eyes almost level with his. "To an extent, Joe, I'm a modern woman, but liberated women have been around for centuries. If I see something I want, if I have to play the aggressor, I will."

"See something you want?" he asked as

his fingers touched her golden hair, as soft as his touch.

"Yes." Her voice was husky.

He bent his head, just a little, and kissed her. A gentle kiss. For all his bluntness, his toughness, Joe could be a gentle man. And he knew, somehow, that women, most of them, do not want to be first-kissed by a vacuum cleaner. That comes later.

She slipped her arms around his waist, then his neck, holding him to her, pressing against him, the kiss gradually intensifying. From the fireplace, they moved to the couch.

She noticed his slight smile. "What's so funny?

He laughed. "Now do we get to do a little old-fashioned smooching and necking?"

She chuckled, her breath hot on his mouth, a breath spiced with wine. "I don't see a thing wrong with that."

Their touches became more intimate, more personal, more demanding. After a time, to the sounds of an unspoken agreement, they silently rose and walked into a bedroom.

They awakened at six the next morning, to the sounds of Joe's clock radio. The announcer had just interrupted his music to inform the public that another body had just been found—beaten, tortured, raped, mutilated, and drowned.

Four

"Fourteen years old!" Erica said, looking at the battered body of Faith Barnett, loathing for the man who would do such a thing evident in her voice. "God!"

"Walked right into the house, snatched her, and carried her away without making a sound," Joe said, shaking his head in disbelief. "Good Christ, what kind of a man are we dealing with?"

"Residuals of chloroform in her lungs," Doctor Williams said, walking into the room from his lab. "I thought it would have to be something like that."

"But how did he get into the house?" Perkins asked. "Is the guy a ghost?"

"He's no ghost," Joe replied, running nervous fingers through his hair. "Seems the Barnetts never lock the back door to their house. The yard is fenced, well lighted at all times, and they keep a trained Doberman inside the fenced area.

"How does someone just walk right past a Doberman?" Perkins shuddered.

"Easily," Erica answered. "If the dog is dead."

Joe held out the mutilated rubber nipple of a baby bottle. "When they work," he said, "they're a very effective silencer. Good for no more than two shots. Depends on the caliber of weapon used. The dog was shot with a twenty-two long rifle hollow point."

Doctor Williams looked at the battered nipple, "I must admit, I've never heard of such a thing."

"They're chancy," Joe said. "If the nipple hole is closed, the weapon can blow up in a man's face."

Erica let her feelings out. "Too bad it didn't."

"Tell me what you've got." Sheriff Roberts sat down heavily in a chair in Joe's office.

"We found where he waited on the side of the hill overlooking the Barnett house. Got some good impressions. He wears a size ten C shoe."

"So do twenty-five million other men," Roberts replied glumly.

"He's about six-feet tall, weighs about one eighty."

"How'd you determine the height?"

"We found where he stood up to use a low limb to balance the rifle. It's just an approximation, T. L., but it is something to go on. When he moved down the hill, his head brushed against the limb; we found some strands of hair. But Doc Williams said he thinks they came from a wig. Williams is sending them to Scientific Analysis Section."

The sheriff nodded. "And?"

"And he smokes a pipe," Erica said.

That brought Roberts's head up, alert. "How do you know that?"

"We found where he parked his car, in a wooded area about a mile from the house. He walked through the woods, stopping once to tap his pipe against a large rock."

"That might be to throw us off."

"Yes, that's a definite possibility," Joe agreed. "But there again, we got lucky. We found fabric strands on a bush. Those were also sent to the crime lab."

"Tire impressions?" the sheriff asked.

"Some good ones, some bad ones. Just like always. And we're not even sure they belong to the car our killer rapist used."

The sheriff stood up, stretching. "Well, you're right about one thing, Joe."

"What's that?"

"It's something to go on."

After Roberts left, Erica said, "The sheriff's been spending a lot of time up on the hill, at Jordan's mansion. The elder Jordan."

"I've noticed."

"Why?" she questioned, as much to herself as to Joe.

"I don't know," he said. "But I sure as hell would like to."

1

"You got no right to roust me!" Chris Northcutt yelled at the officers standing in his living room in the cabin in the hills above Red Bay/Denton. "I'm clean. I ain't done one goddamn thing!"

"No one has accused you of doing anything," Erica reminded him. "We just want to talk with you. You can order us to leave if you wish."

"And if I do, I get hauled in for spitting on the sidewalk, and you really get to talk to me." He laughed, calming down. "Aw, hell, have a seat and ask your questions."

"Do you want me to read you your rights?" Joe asked.

Northcutt again laughed. "Rights? Are you kidding? Hell, I know them better than you do. Come on, you people got a sheet on me, so knock off the bullshit and get to the point. What'd you want with me?"

Erica started to read him his rights; he waved her silent. "I know them; I waive them. Just ask your goddamn questions and then get out, leave me alone.

"Where were you last night, between ten p.m. and two a.m.?" Joe asked.

"In town, at Neal's Bar 'til about midnight. I know, I know, I'm still on parole and I'm not supposed to drink. But I did, and I do, so BFD."

Erica looked at him. "What?"

"Big Fuckin' Deal," Northcutt replied.

"How quaint," she muttered.

"And after that?" Joe asked, a faint smile on his lips at Erica's expression.

"I grabbed a sandwich and a cup of coffee at the all-night cafe on Twelfth Street and talked with the counterman for a few minutes, then came straight here and watched TV."

Joe nodded at Erica and she went outside to the car to call in to dispatch, to have his story checked as much as possible.

When the door had closed, Northcutt said, "Davis? Look, I don't like what's happening' around here either, man. And I mean that."

Joe said nothing, hoping Northcutt would volunteer something, *anything,* that would help them, for Joe didn't believe the ex-con was guilty of the rapes and murders. It was only a cop's hunch, but in many instances, that was all a cop had to go on.

"I know," Northcutt said, "I did time for

rape." His smile was bitter. "The same woman, twice. If that makes any sense to you. But I'm telling you the same thing I told the judge, the jury, and my lawyer—it wasn't rape. I never raped nobody—ever! I never marked her, never hit her, never forced her into doing nothing.

"Let me ask *you* this—how come *she* was never put on the polygraph? How come *she* didn't have to take no PSE test? How come the findings on *me* weren't allowed in court? I come out clean on all the tests the cops gave me."

Joe nodded his agreement, for he had read the jacket on Chris Northcutt, and felt the man had been shafted into prison. Rape was an ugly charge—hard to prove, embarrassing for the victim and marking both victim and rapist for life.

Fuckee and fuckor, as one hard-nosed St. Louis cop had once referred to victim and assailant.

"I come out of that hellhole of a prison a hard and bitter man, Davis. Oh, I wasn't no angel before I went in, but I wasn't no hard case, either."

Erica returned. "He's clean. His story checks out. One of our patrolmen saw him in both places."

Joe nodded. "I felt his story would hold up." He looked at Northcutt. "Can you, will you, help us on this one?"

"What the hell can I do?"

"Listen. Keep your eyes and ears open. Report to me if you hear anything."

"Be a snitch for you?" The ex-con grinned. "Ain't that something, now?"

"Will you?" Joe pressed.

Northcutt shrugged. "Sure, why not? Listen, both of you: now, I may be telling you things you already know, but I'm gonna say it, anyway. You guys ain't dealin' with no average stick-it-in-and-run artist. This dude is bent 'way out of shape—sexually. I been hearin' talk around town 'bout some of the things that was done to the girls, and if it's true you guys got yourselves a real twisto to deal with. He's so smart he's crazy. He ain't carryin' half a load—he's overloaded!"

"What have you heard?" Erica asked.

"Well, that—" Northcutt shifted his eyes from Joe to Erica. "Man, I don't feel right talkin' 'bout this in front of her!"

"She's a cop, Chris. Go ahead."

"Well, street talk is this dude's made some of these girls go down on him. You know, suck him off. If I was a woman, I'd bite that bastard's wang clean off! That don't follow the pattern of any rape artist I talked to in the bucket. I ain't tryin' to tell you people your business, but it seems to me that these gals *know* this dude, and trust him, you know? Trust him to keep his word, like maybe he's tellin' them he'll let them go after they . . . you know."

"Yeah, we've thought of that," Joe said. "That's the way I see it, too. Anything else?"

"That he's started carvin' on them. That true?" Joe nodded. "And there's something else, too. These gals is all rich bitches from the Hill Section." He looked at Joe and Erica. Their faces were noncommittal. Northcutt chuckled. "Yeah, I bet you guys is sittin' on some facts you're not releasin', ain't you? Well, just remember this: if *I* can put it all together, so will them smartass press boys, sooner or later."

"Have you told anyone else of your theory?" Joe asked.

Chris shook his head. "Naw. You guys got it bad enough without a bunch of amateurs jumpin' in, muddyin' up the waters."

"We appreciate that," Erica said, and meant it. She realized that Northcutt was no fool.

The big ex-con frowned. "I hope you guys catch this weirdo pretty soon. He's a bad one. Kinky. And I got a feelin' he's gonna get worse as he goes along."

"So do we," Joe said.

2

Joe and Erica cruised the streets and alleys of Red Bay and Denton that Saturday night, riding in Joe's personal car, an un-marked Mercury. They looked for anything and anybody out of the ordinary; something or someone that might spark a clue from the dry tinder of evidence they had gathered. They, along with a double shift at the station, many patrolmen working on their own time, had kept the computers humming around the state and parts of the U.S. all day, checking out every possible suspect; every person, male or female, who had moved into the area during the past five years. They had drawn a blank at almost every turn.

Dave Hicks was at the top of the suspect list, followed by Martin Sterling. Each was just a shade over five-ten, and weighed between one sixty-five and one-eighty. Each smoked a pipe. Nothing could be proven on Hicks, past or present. Sterling had a sheet on him of window-peeping, attempted child-molesting, and assault, but it was an old jacket. He had been clean for years, married and settled down.

The hair they had found on the hill over-looking the Barnett house was from a wig. No help there. The pieces of fabric had not yet been returned from the upstate crime lab.

"We're missing something," Erica said, gazing out the window at the shops on Main

Street. "It's right before our noses, so close we can't see it."

"I get the same vibes," Joe replied, his eyes constantly roaming the streets, looking. "Northcutt was right, Erica. The girls knew this fellow. Trusted him. Hicks?"

"Maybe, but he's checked out right so far. Sterling? No. He just doesn't fit. The court-ordered psychiatrist he saw following his trouble in the city says he's straight. He's been clean for years. Maybe there's two of them, Joe—ever think of that?"

"Two warped personalities coming together. Rare, in cases like these."

"But do you want to toss that idea out the window?"

Joe sighed. "No. We'd better kick it around."

At ten o'clock, the police radio began blaring an All Points Bulletin: Ginger Kennedy was missing.

Erica summed up their feelings. "Aw, shit!"

3

It was a gritty-eyed and grim Sunday morning for the sheriff's department of Morrison County. Fifteen-year-old Ginger Kennedy had been found at dawn, hanging from a rusty meathook in an old, deserted meatpacking plant on the edge of Red Bay. Like the others before her, Ginger had been beaten, tortured, raped, mutilated, and drowned. A rope had been looped around her ankles, binding them, and she had been left hanging, head down, on the hook, her long blonde hair touching the dirty floor, matted in a thickening puddle of blood.

"All girls," Erica said quietly to Joe as the body of Ginger was gently lowered to the floor. The pictures had been taken of the crime scene, the area checked for prints, barriers erected around the building to keep the curious away.

"What?" Joe looked at her.

"All girls," Erica repeated. "I'll buy your theory a hundred percent, now, Joe. And I think it's time we went to see Sheriff Roberts."

"He's gonna throw us right out of his office," he warned.

He was very nearly correct.

"You're full of shit!" T. L. Roberts bluntly told his ace detective.

"Will you hear me out before you start yelling at me?" Joe asked.

Sheriff Roberts glared at him for a few seconds, then nodded his head minutely.

For ten minutes, Joe outlined his theory in detail, leaving nothing out, while the sheriff leaned back in his swivel chair, his face impassive. He did grunt and nod in several places, negatively or positively—neither Joe nor Erica could be sure.

Erica watched the sheriff's face, a slow sensation of distrust sweeping over her. Joe had told her the night before that Roberts knew more about the Evans murders than he was telling, or had ever told. *Why?* she had asked. *A hunch,* Joe had replied. Now she believed Joe.

How did you reach that conclusion? she asked herself.

A hunch, the silent voice replied.

When Joe finished, T. L. sat for a full minute, his gaze shifting from man to woman. Finally, he said, "I oughta throw you both out of this office for dumping this grief on me. You know that?"

Joe leaned forward, his hands on the sheriff's desk. "But what I said does have a ring of truth to it, doesn't it, T. L.?"

Reluctantly, grudgingly, the sheriff admitted that, yes, it did. "But you've had a hard-on for Howard Jordan for years, Joe. You two are like a dog and a cat walking around each other. And you despise Howard Junior."

"But I've never rousted him, or any of the other Eleven in all the years I've been on the department. Have I, T. L.?"

"Not to my knowledge."

"Not good enough, sheriff," Joe corrected. "You know I haven't. And I could have, many times with legal justification."

Joe looked deeply into the sheriff's eyes, his hunch that Roberts was holding something back growing stronger in his mind. But what?

"All right, Joe, what do you want me to do?" Roberts asked.

"Let me find out what happened to Paul Evans."

"Joe, come on! Hell, that was twenty-five years ago. Where in the hell would we start? Damn, why don't you just drop this idea and come back to reality?"

Joe ignored that and opened a folder he had brought into the sheriff's office. "I know where to start, T. L." he said. "The only railroad line that ran close to Bell Lake—it crosses the lake at the south end— this is twenty-five years ago, remember, was the old Red River line, long out of business. It had a straight run to Joplin. Let me find out if anybody, any cop, saw Paul that next day. What do we have to lose, T. L.?"

"My sanity," the sheriff said, stabbing at humor that didn't quite make it. "Why a train?"

"Just a hunch. The lake was dragged, wasn't it?"

"Hell, yes, it was dragged!" Roberts said hotly.

"Well?" Joe asked.

"All right. All right. Check it out. When you find you're barking up a dead tree, come back and work on the 'Graduation Murders.' "

"The what?" Erica asked.

"That's what our local press boys have begun calling them." Roberts flipped open a newspaper on his desk. He pushed the paper across the desk. "Read all about it," he said with absolutely no humor in his voice.

Both Joe and Erica noticed the sheriff had begun aging badly.

4

"You wanna know *what*, lieutenant?" the voice of Joe's counterpart in Joplin was full of incredulity. "Jesus Christ, man—twenty-six years ago!?"

"You know the troubles we're having over here," Joe reminded the man. "Come on, we're grabbing at straws, lieutenant. Help us if you can."

"A twenty-five-year-old clue is that important to you, Joe?"

"Yes, it is."

"It'll be tomorrow afternoon, Joe. At the earliest."

"Say, two o'clock?" Joe pressed for a time.

A long sigh from Joplin. "Okay, Joe—two o'clock it is."

5

The mayors of Denton and Red Bay met with their city councils to discuss a curfew. It was voted down; this was tourist season, and the communities stood to lose hundreds of thousands of dollars if such action were to go into effect. The local newspaper, a daily serving both towns, was told, through its editor, to play down the events, unless it wanted to lose a full fifty percent of its advertising—immediately. The local radio station was also cautioned to cool it. *Without tourism, we're dead,* the editor and station manager were reminded. *So play it down.*

Hardware and sporting goods stores in Morrison County quickly sold out of handguns. All high school graduation parties were cancelled—on a middle and lower class level, that is—the more affluent could, and did, hire special guards for their kids' parties.

The murders only seemed to increase tourism, as the curious came in to gawk and stare and wonder. And the community was quiet for a few days. As the editor of the newspaper told Joe: "Under the quiet, an armed camp."

6

"Joe?" the police lieutenant spoke through long lines from Joplin. "We lucked up—and I mean lucked up. I'll send it on the wire. Hope it'll do you some good, 'cause there ain't no more. Good luck, pal."

Joe waited by the teletype and felt an icy chill move over him as the printer began its message.

From report of Patrolman Charles Mumford (now dead) June 1973, Joplin, MO PD. Mumford searching boxcars at RR Depot reported seeing boy, approx age 12 or 13, run from caboose. Mumford startled at boy's appearance. Boy had serious head wound. Head badly swollen. Mumford stated: Boy scared the crap out of him! Never seen anything alive that looked like that.

Mumford chased boy down RR tracks, to the West. Boy outran Mumford.

End report from Joplin PD.

The teleprinter began clattering as other PD's and sheriff's department reports came in. The Joplin PD lieutenant had worked half the night, calling westward, seeking information.

Stand by to receive more transmissions . . .

. . . . .

Wichita PD reports old file on boy with serious head wound reported seen on afternoon June 1973. Boy jumped from boxcar. RR Detectives chased him and lost him. Sheriff's Deputies picked up trail and chased boy into woods. Lost him. Report kept open cause thought boy was kidnapping victim April 1973.

Stand by for further transmissions. . . .

. . . .

Salina KS PD reports old file on kidnap. Boy with serious head wound reported stealing clothes from clothesline. Housewife fainted at sight of him, called sheriff's department. Boy gone when deputies arrived. Approx age of boy 12 or 13. Thin. Badly hurt.

Stand by to receive more transmissions. . . .

. . . . .

To: Joe Davis Morrison Ct Sheriff's Dept.

From: Hays KS PD. Dodge City PD. Lamar CO PD. Colo Springs PD.

Old files on young boy with head wound dated 6/20/73, 6/25/73, 6/27/73, 6/30/73. Heading West. Good hunting, Joe. You're on old cold trail.

End transmissions on boy/head wound.

Before Joe could get away from the teleprinter, the machine began rattling.

To Joe Davis, Morrison Ct Sheriff's Dept.
From FBI, Kansas City MO.
Reading your transmissions. Sorry—didn't mean snoop. Why interest in boy with head wound, 1973? May we be of assistance? Special Agent Wainwright.

Joe keyed the teleprinter and tapped out:

Believe boy tied in with rash of rape/murders occurring in Denton-

Red Bay area. Any help appreciated.
Davis out.

From FBI: Give us thirty minutes,
Joe. Will get back if any info avail.
Punching into computers. Wainwright.

Twenty minutes later:

Joe—suggest you call FBI office, Denver,
CO. May have something for you. Good
hunting and keep us informed if we can
be of any further help. Wainwright, FBI
KC.

Joe called the Denver office of the FBI, Erica
by his side. He recorded the conversation, smiling as he did so. Erica listened to the playback,
kissed Joe on the mouth, and together they
walked into Sheriff Roberts's office.

Sheriff Roberts listened to the playback,
his face tightening with each word. Erica
and Joe watched the sheriff, each wonder-
ing what was wrong with him.

"So here's what we've got, Joe," the agent
in Denver said. "Seems the Denver PD
picked up a small boy, 'bout thirteen or
fourteen years old, back in '73. Massive
head wound. Had been beaten badly. All
over his body. The PD got him off a freight

train, heading west. We were called in because we were working a kidnap out of Kansas from back in April, same year.

"The boy did not know who he was or where he came from or where he was going or how or who inflicted the wounds upon him. He was taken to a local hospital. Stayed there for months. Underwent several operations. We dropped out of the case after finding the original kidnap victim dead back in Kansas. The boy—John Doe—gained a lot of weight and height. Just before he was to be handed over to juvenile authorities, he skipped out. Hasn't been seen or heard of since. How does this kid tie in with what's happening in your area?"

"I think this boy is Paul Evans. I think he's back, and I think he's the man doing the raping and killing here."

The agent whistled. "You got yourself a big job, Joe."

"Don't I know it."

"Any kidnap notes, ransom, taking them across state lines, any minorities involved, proven civil rights violations?"

"No, to all your questions."

"Wish we could help."

"Me, too. Thanks for your help on this one, partner."

"Keep me informed, Joe."

"Will do."

Sheriff Roberts sighed, running his fingers through his gray, thinning hair. "Joe, you've got something here. But I'm not sure what."

"Goddammit, T. L.!"

"Sit down!" Roberts ordered. "Now, just get hold of yourself. Think a minute, man. You have a twenty-six-year-old report, or reports, of a boy with a head wound. He was first spotted in Joplin, heading west. He—"

"It's Paul Evans!" Joe shouted, slamming both hands on the sheriff's desk.

Outside, in the squad room, all heads turned; the clatter of typewriters ceased; personnel fell silent.

"Prove it!" Roberts roared, jumping to his feet, glaring.

"I will." Joe returned the glare. "I will. Yes, sir, I'll damn sure do that little thing."

"Don't screw up!" the sheriff warned him. "Don't bring any lawsuits on this department just because you've got old memories that won't heal."

"I heard that, T. L.," Joe said. Then he whirled around and stalked out the door, Erica right behind him.

They did not see Sheriff Roberts pick up the phone, dialing a number.

PAUL

His first assignment took him to a small town in Oregon, where he stayed for a time, perfecting his new vocation. He then went to the suburbs of St. Louis, where he stayed for a few years, becoming active in volunteer work, working with a suicide prevention group, and helping to deal with mentally disturbed people. Then, with a smile on his lips, he heard of an opening in Red Bay.

After talking with his sister/wife, he took the new assignment and they settled right in.

Paul, and his sister/wife.

Five

Joe took his frustrations out on Erica that night, during their lovemaking, at her home, going at her savagely. He held back ejaculation for what seemed to her like hours, while she experienced one shattering climax after another. When he finally filled her, she held him, listening to his ragged breathing calm and his heart slow its wild pounding.

"Many more of those, Joe," she said, kissing his nose, "and I won't be able to walk and you'll probably have a heart attack. I've never experienced anything like that."

That brought a grin from him. "Would you like for me to offer an apology?"

"Certainly not!" She laughed. "Do make it a point to argue with the sheriff at least once a week, will you?"

He was silent for a time, content to lie with her close to him, enjoying the warmth of her skin against his. Then he suddenly cursed and reached for the phone by the bed, hurriedly dialing a number.

"Doc? Sorry to bother you at this late hour."

"Then why did you?" the old ME popped back.

Joe expected and ignored the smart retort. "Doc, the stomach contents of the girls: city water or lake water?"

The ME cursed for a long time. "Goddammit, Joe! I told the sheriff. Lake water."

"Well, he damn sure didn't tell me!"

A long pause on the other end of the connection. "Are you certain?"

"You're damn right I'm certain. What is it with Roberts, anyway, Doc? He's behaving funny as hell."

"Maybe he's got a lot on his mind?"

"Maybe he's covering something up?"

"Serious charge. Better make damn sure you can prove it if you repeat it to anyone else."

"I don't intend to repeat it to anyone else. And I'm sure you'll keep it to yourself."

"I've forgotten it already. Now perhaps you'll allow an old man to go back to sleep? Where are you—over there humping that goodlooking Norwegian gal?"

"Doc." Joe laughed. "You're a dirty old man."

"Of course I am." He hung up.

Joe told Erica the other side of his conversation.

"Why would Roberts hold back information?" she questioned. "Surely he would know we'd find out."

"I don't know. But I'm not going to say anything about it to him."

"Bell Lake is miles long, Joe. Are you thinking our boy takes the girls out there, does his thing, then drowns them?"

"Maybe. Maybe he owns a camp on the lake."

"Lots of people own camps out there, Joe."

"Yeah, including Howard Jordan."

"How could we patrol it?"

"We couldn't. Impossible. There are dozens of roads leading in and out. Lodges and hotels and motels. We've run checks on all the employees out there, as you well know. Nothing. Not one goddamn thing!"

They lay still for a time, all passion sated. She rested her head on his shoulder, her arm across his bare stomach. Her breath was warm on his skin. "Joe, if it really is Paul Evans, wouldn't someone have recognized him by now? Surely *someone* in this area knew him that well."

Joe was thinking of the woman he had seen from time to time, in Red Bay; he had seen her once or twice a month for years. Something about her triggered a peculiar flash of memory within him . . . something about her walk, her bearing, that was somehow familiar to him. She was a nice lady, married to a nice fellow, and Joe's feelings toward her were not sexual, not at all. But there was something—

"No," he returned to the present, "I don't believe so." His breathing and heartbeat were normal, calm finally, after the hour of furious lovemaking. "The Evans family had only lived here for three years. You may have missed that in the report. They moved here from California. The only reason Paul was invited to join the group was because of Howard's hots for Paul's sister. Paul would be a middle-aged man by now—or approaching it." That was said ruefully. "A mustache, hair style. No, I don't believe anyone would recognize him."

Erica stiffened beside him; Joe could feel the tension in her. "Joe? What you just said: California."

"What of it?" He yawned hugely. Then the implication of her words hit him and he sat up in bed. "California! Sure. Paul didn't know who he was or where he was going or what had happened to him, but instinct carried him westward." He started to rise. Strong hands brought him back to the sheets.

"No way," Erica said, authority in her voice. "Not tonight. It's almost midnight. There will be plenty of time tomorrow." She glanced at the digital clock on the bedside stand. "Or I should say today." It was just past midnight.

He smiled at her in the semi-darkness of the bedroom. "And, my dear, just how do you plan on keeping me here? I couldn't get another erection with the help of a block and tackle."

Her fingers grasped his penis and squeezed gently but firmly. She laughingly mocked him. "Now, my dear, would you like to try jumping out of bed?"

He shook his head. "I think I'll spend the night."

"Wise choice, my dear."

"I heard that."

1

The few threads of fabric found on the hill overlooking the Barnett house were returned from the crime lab. There again, the detectives struck out: the shirt was a cheap sport shirt, made in Taiwan and sold locally in a dozen stores, nationally in thousands of stores.

"Damn!" Joe said. "Why couldn't it have come from Cable Car Clothiers, or some other highfalutin' company?"

Erica looked at him and laughed. "Highfalutin', Joe?"

Reporters from the national networks

picked up on the Graduation Murders and converged on the Red Bay/Denton area. They hung around for two days, asking questions, but nothing happened. The killer was in his lair, waiting for the limelight to shut off. By Thursday afternoon, with no new murder/rapes to report, the press pulled out. Many people thought the killer had left, and began making plans for a huge party that Friday night.

"This is what he's been waiting for," Erica said to Sheriff Roberts and Joe.

The sheriff agreed. "I'm putting everybody I've got in the field this weekend. The state police is sending in twenty-five men to take some of the strain off us. I hope to God we can keep the lid on tight."

"Don't put any money on that," Joe said.

The sheriff looked at him, a strange light in his eyes. The light faded. "You're such a joy and comfort to me."

Joe allowed a tight grin to crease his lips. "Thanks. Oh, T. L.?"

The sheriff turned around. "Yes?"

"Why didn't you tell me about the lake water in the girls' stomachs?"

The sheriff's face reddened. "I—ah—forgot, that's all."

Joe met the older man's gaze with unblinking eyes. Roberts finally dropped his eyes. "T. L.? What are you holding back from me?"

"Not a goddamn thing!" He whirled around and walked down the hall, muttering.

"He's lying," Erica said.

"I heard that, babe. But *why?*"

"How long has he been a widower, Joe?"

"Six years. Why?"

"Just curious. Does Roberts own a camp on the lake?"

The two detectives looked at each other for a few seconds. Joe nodded slowly. "Yes, he does."

PAUL

"Why on earth would you want to do such a thing?" the man asked the woman.

"Butt out!" she told him harshly, her voice muffled through the bandages covering her face. "Just let me die."

"No, you're not going to die. Won't you at least tell me your name?"

"Fuck you!"

"I'm only trying to help."

"Why?"

"Because it's my job, because I want to help you. Who are you? How did you hurt yourself?"

She laughed at him, a bitter laugh, as memories swirled through her brain, returning to her in a cloud of pain and hate. She remembered the struggle in her apartment, the pain in her head as a hard fist slammed against her jaw, dropping her to the carpet. She remembered seeing the foot draw back, to kick her again and again in the face, and the sounds of her facial bones crunching as they were shattered by the kicks. She remembered being dragged from a car, and the brief struggle in the rain, then that long fall until she exploded into a vortex of colors, finally drifting into blackness; soft, wet darkness.

"What is your name?" the man persisted.

"I'm nobody. I've never been anybody, and I plan to remain that way." She touched her face, swathed in bandages. her left arm was in a heavy cast and her right arm hurt, but was functional. "My face must be a mess. Do you know what happened?"

"I suppose the same thing that happened to your legs. Do you want to tell me about it?"

She hesitated, only fragments of what happened swirling in her brain, mingled with that moment of empty space, the terrible sensation of having nothing firm under her feet. She turned her eyes to look at the man beside her bed in the hospital. "Where was I found?"

"Some kids found you by the side of the road. They called the police, and the ambulance brought you here. That was four days ago."

Four days! "I've been unconscious all that time? Did I say anything?"

"Yes, you've been unconscious for four days. And, no, you said nothing."

"I can't move my legs."

"They were broken, but you're going to be all right, I assure you."

"Is my face very bad?"

"Yes," he told her honestly. "Surgery will be required when you grow stronger. But the doctors don't know what you looked like before your—accident. They don't really know how to repair your face."

"I don't have any money for all that."

"The organization I work for has a fund. Don't worry about it."

"What you said before, I mean . . . the doctors can't make me look like I did before my accident?"

"That is correct."

She smiled under her bandages. "Good."

2

"Quiet." Erica spoke to relieve the monotonous silence in the car.

Behind the wheel, Joe smiled. "Not much of a conversationalist tonight, am I, babe?"

But one hell of a lover, she thought. "Understatement of the week." She smiled at him but Joe was not in a humorous mood.

"He's out there." He cut his eyes to the passing darkness, a few yards on either side of the street lamps. "And he's waiting. Just waiting to strike again."

"The entire department is on patrol tonight, Joe," she reminded her partner. "With twenty-five state troopers added. I can't believe this guy'd be stupid enough to try anything tonight."

"He's not stupid, Erica, and you know it. He's crazy, but he's also smart as hell. And everybody in this community knows him. No one suspects him. That's got to be the way is it. It's got to be!"

She sighed in frustration. "As much as I hate to admit it, I think you're right."

3

"Mike," the girl said, frightened. "You gotta get this car started and get us outta here. My parents will kill me if they find out we left the party to go parking. God, Mike! What if *he's* out there?"

"Dammit, Laura," the oldest Wooten boy said, impatiently, "I'm *trying* to get it started. I tell you, we're out of gas!"

There was disgust in her voice, "Mike, that's the oldest trick in the book. Now, come on, Mike! Start the car and let's get *out* of here."

He put his forehead on the steering wheel and sighed with great teenage weariness. "Lisa used my car this afternoon to go riding around. Boy, she sure rode around, didn't she? Used a half a tank of gas. I'm sorry, Laura, I shoulda checked the gauge. But I didn't."

Laura Richard put her hand on his arm. "I'm sorry, Mike. I didn't mean to yell at you, I really didn't. I just got scared for a minute, that's all. Look, we're in the park. It isn't like we're 'way out in the country, or something, you know? Look—" she said, pointing, "you can just see the pay phone by the civil war monument. Go call Phil's Service Station and get them to bring us some gas. They'll do it. I'll lock all the doors while you're gone."

Doubt was in his eyes, fear in his voice. The park was very dark. "You'll be all right here?"

She laughed at him, then kissed him. "Sure, I will." She gave him a little push. "Go on. The faster you move the quicker we'll get out of here."

She locked the doors behind him and watched him melt into the darkness of the park. Putting her arms under her breasts, she shivered, although the night was pleasant in Missouri. Somewhere in the park a night bird called, receiving no reply. The park was silent. *Just like a graveyard,* Laura thought, then quickly pushed that thought from her. *Hurry up,* Mike, she mentally urged him. *Please hurry.*

When the man stepped out of the shadows in the park, Mike Wooten felt a few drops of urine wet his underwear shorts. Through his fear, he was embarrassed. His heart was beating wildly, pounding in his chest.

"Oh, my Lord, sir!" he gasped out after recognizing the man. "You scared me bad, sir, you really did. Wow!" He tried to laugh.

"Now, now," the man calmed the boy. "Settle down, now. Are you having some sort of trouble, Mike?"

"Yes, sir. Me and . . . uh"—he was clearly embarrassed—"Laura was parked . . . uh . . . over there." He pointed. The car could not be seen through the timber in the park. "I guess I ran out of gas. I really did, sir." He grinned. "I was going to the phone to call the service station."

The man's face and words were stern, lashing at the teenager with vocal and silent rebuke. "Mike, you know better than to park out here. Anywhere, for that matter."

"Yes, sir. I am sorry. Believe me, I am."

"Well, all right, then, You go on back to the car and stay with Laura. I'll call the service station. Go on, now."

"Yes, sir," Mike said, turning around. His head exploded in pain as something smashed against his skull. He fell to his knees, hands working in agony on the sidewalk, bloodying his palms and knuckles. Another blow to the head and he fell face forward, smashing his nose and mouth on the concrete, dying in the park. Mercifully, he did not see nor feel the tire iron as it bludgeoned his face into a mass of shiny blood, bone, and tissue. The man struck him again and again, beating the boy until his arm was weary. Mike's face was pounded into pulp, smashed beyond recognition, his brains splattering the sidewalk.

The man shoved the bloody tire iron behind his belt and walked to the car in the darkness.

Laura almost screamed when he tapped on the window. Then she relaxed, grinning at his familiar and trusting smile. She rolled down the window.

"Hi. We missed you at the dance this evening. Heard you weren't feeling well. How are you?"

"Much better, thanks." He put his hand on the door.

"What are you doing out here at this time of night?" she asked, a touch of fear crawling up her spine.

"Volunteer watch," he said, his words soothing her fears. "I saw Mike in the park just as he was phoning for help." The man smiled. "Or, I should say, trying to phone. He didn't have a dime on him."

Laura laughed. "That's so like him."

"A police car came by and we flagged it down. It's waiting for us by the phone booth." He held out his hand. "Come on, I'll walk with you through the park."

She willingly, eagerly, jumped out of the car and looked up at him just in time to catch a hard fist on the jaw. She dropped to the gravel, stunned. He hit her again, expertly, just behind the ear, plunging her into unconsciousness.

He ran his hands over her body, squeezing her breasts, slipping his hand up her dress, touching her legs, her panties, her pubic area. He began breathing harshly as he felt an erection grow.

When Laura awakened, she was in the backseat of a car, on the floorboards, covered with a blanket. Her hands and feet were tied, and she could not move. Her mouth was taped shut, and there was a bag of some sort over her head.

She began to weep, silently.

She rode for a short distance—no more, she guessed, than two or three miles, maybe four. When the car stopped she was pulled rudely, roughly, from the backseat and dragged across the ground, up some steps, bruising her, and into a house. She was dragged down some steps, into a musty smelling place. A basement, she guessed, and she was correct.

"Strip her!" a woman's voice ordered. A familiar voice. "I want to see her pretty little cunt."

Hands were on her, tearing the clothes from her. Cool air fanned her nakedness. The man's hands roamed her body, squeezing and hurting her. Fingers plunged past the dryness, penetrating her, working in and out.

"I want to hear her scream," the woman said. "Remove the tape from her mouth."

A hand jerked the tape painfully from her lips, but the sack remained over her head.

And then the pain began as he spread her legs, positioned himself, and tore into her. His hands hurt her breasts, clamping down brutally.

Through her screaming, Laura could hear the woman laughing insanely.

And then the unspeakable things were done to her. And the night wore painfully, slowly, onward.

4

It was one o'clock Saturday morning before Mike's Chevy was found. Another ten minutes ticked past before his gruesome remains were discovered. One local deputy lost his supper when he looked at the almost headless body. At one thirty, the park resembled an electric light circus, the blue and red whirling strobes reflecting wildly from the many trees and bushes and sidewalks.

Sergeant Carter of the Missouri Highway Patrol watched as Joe and Erica walked up the sidewalk to the body, his eyes not so much on Joe as on Erica's lushness. A good cop, Sergeant Carter nevertheless had an eye for the ladies. And this, he reflected, was one hell of a lady. But, he observed sadly, taking in the way she looked at Joe, she was private property.

"Joe. Miss Johansen. People, I've worked killer wrecks that weren't this bad. You folks have got a real flake on your hands this time."

"Don't we know it," Joe said, kneeling down beside the blanket-covered body of the young man. His shoes just touched the thickening puddle of blood that spread around the body. He lifted the blanket and took a long look at the grisly sight. *Flake, is right,* he thought. *A real psycho. Took a hell of a lot of licks to do this.* "Found the murder weapon?"

"Not yet."

"One of those blunt instrument reports, Joe?" he was asked.

"What else?" Joe said. "How about an ID?"

"Positive," Carter replied. "Michael Vincent Wooten. Seventeen. Senior at Denton High. Had a date with Laura Richard. The car is over there." He jerked his thumb.

"Any sign of her?" Erica asked. She knew the answer to her question before the big trooper opened his mouth.

"No, ma'am," Carter said.

"Look over here, Joe," a deputy called. "See what you can make of this."

A section of ground on the passenger side of Mike's Chevy had been roped off, crime scene posters hanging on the ropes. The gravel around the area was disturbed, slashed and marked by what appeared to be panicked footsteps. A bright spot of blood on the pea-gravel caught Joe's eye.

"Cut her hand when she fell, maybe?" he asked.

"That's the way I see it."

Off near the rope's edge, an earring gleamed dully among the gravel.

"Somebody jerked her out of the car, or she got out willingly and then panicked, maybe he hit her," Joe conjectured. "When she fell, she cut her hand and lost an earring. Seal this area off until dawn, then go over it carefully. Find out where he parked his car, if you can. We've got those impressions of the tires behind the Barnett house.

Maybe we'll get lucky." He looked up at Carter. "APB gone out on this girl?"

"Sure," the trooper said, adding, "for all the good it'll do."

"You want us to fan out, chase any kids we find off the street?" a deputy asked.

"If you can find any, yes. But I think our boy's done his work for this night." He looked at another deputy. "First thing this morning, Jimmy, get a team together. Go to every service station, every tire shop, in the area. Get a list of everyone who bought new tires in the past two weeks. Bring the list to me, and tell the tire people to hold their trade-ins."

"Yes, sir."

Joe waited until all pictures were taken of the crime area, then carefully picked up the earring and put it in a clear plastic evidence bag. He stood up. "All right, let's go look for what's left of Laura Richard."

"Why not ask the sheriff?" a state trooper walked up, a hat in his hand.

All heads turned to look at the highway cop and the cowboy hat in his hand.

"Why ask the sheriff?" Joe inquired.

"I found this Stetson right over there," the trooper said. "It's got T. L. Roberts on the sweatband."

Six

"Holy shit!" a deputy said, his eyes on the sheriff's familiar Stetson.

"Sorry to disappoint you," Joe said, "but that hat was stolen out of T. L.'s car a couple of months ago. He bitched about it for a week. Look at it. That hat's been lyin' out there for several days. It's weather-worn."

The trooper grinned ruefully. "I'm glad to hear that, Joe. But I sure thought I had something for a while."

"Let's go to work, people," Joe said.

Laura was found just after dawn, in a deserted house on the outskirts of Red Bay. But this time the police got lucky: a bum had found her. He had been asleep in the old house, and had seen the man who put her there. The police had an eye-witness.

* * *

1

Joe read Doc Williams's report carefully, then looked up at the old ME. "Lake water, but *old* lake water, doc?"

"Yes. Some organisms in the water are dying, oxygen is gone. It isn't fresh lake water. It wouldn't hold up in court, though, Joe. A smart defender would tear it all to shreds."

"So what you're saying is our boy's got himself a big barrel of lake water hidden somewhere, using that to drown his victims in?"

"I would say so, yes. But there's more. When Laura was drowned, she fought, naturally. She sucked in a lot of water, and also some hair that wasn't hers. Perkins says, tentatively speaking, the hair samples match Ruth Jordan's hair. So yes, he's drowned at least two in the same barrel, or container."

"Can we take that to court?" Erica asked.

"After we get a confirmation from the state crime lab, yes."

Joe rubbed his unshaven face and aching eyes. "Nine murders and eight rapes," he said, more to himself than to the others in the room. He glanced at Erica. "Has the old vag calmed down enough to talk yet?"

The vagrant had been asleep in the house when Laura's body was carried in and placed not three feet from where he was hiding behind an old chair. The bum had been frightened half out of his wits.

"Just barely," Erica replied, looking as fresh as if she had just stepped out of a hot bath after a full eight hours of sleep. Only a slight darkness under her eyes betrayed her weariness. "We got him calmed down enough to eat, and he hasn't stopped eating since. We finally had to take the plate out from under his nose. Told him he wouldn't get anything else to eat until he took a shower. That man smells like a stockyard in July."

"What'd he say to that?" Doc Williams asked.

Erica smiled. "Asked me if I'd take a shower with him."

"And you said. . . ?" Joe asked.

"I told him to put his suggestion where the sun don't shine."

Williams laughed.

Joe grinned, and rose stiffly from his chair, the joints in his knees popping. "Well, let's go see him. Maybe he can help us break this case."

"You gotta pertec' me!" the old vagrant said, his eyes still wild with fear. "I'll tell ya whut I seen, but you gotta promise to pertec' me. Man, I seen whut he done to that girl, and her cold and dead, too!"

Joe stirred at his words. "What did he do to her, Mr. Jones?" The vagrant had told them his name was Joe Smith, then Joe Dokes, finally John Jones.

"You gonna make me take a bath?" the old man asked sourly.

"If you stay in this jail you'll take a bath," Joe told him. "What did he do to the girl?"

"Maybe I changed my mind 'bout tellin' you anythang?" A sly look sprang into his eyes.

Joe was unruffled. He looked at Erica. "How much money did Mr. Jones have on him when he asked for protective custody?"

"One dollar and fifteen cents, and no visible means of support."

"Book him," Joe stood up. "Then mug him and print him. Run him through the FBI. That shouldn't take more than three weeks. Then call some deputies and toss him in the shower, hose him down good."

"Wait a minute! Lord, man, I was just funnin' with you. That's all. Whut do you wanna know?"

"Start from the beginning, when you woke up and the man was carrying the girl into the house. What then?"

The vagrant dropped his eyes. "He done it to her. You know."

"I don't know, Mr. Jones. What do you mean: 'He done it to her?' "

"You gonna make me say it in front of her?" he cut his eyes to Erica.

"Say it, Mr. Jones."

"Well, damn you, then! He done it to her. Plopped 'er down on the floor, spread her legs, pulled out his pecker, and screwed her!"

"The man had an erection immediately?" Erica asked calmly.

"Lord! Whut kind of woman are you?" the old man asked. "No! He played with hisself fer a while first."

"He masturbated, you mean?" she asked.

"Women shore have come along ways," the old man muttered. "Yeah, he jacked hisself off fer a minute 'er two, mumbling all the time."

"What was he mumbling?" Joe asked, alert.

"Crazy stuff. First hit were the Bible, then he would cuss. Then he said something 'bout Judy somebody-or-the-other. Then he flung hisself on her and done it to her."

"What size would you say his erection was?" Erica asked. "The length."

"Good Lord, lady!"

"It's important that we know, Mr. Jones," Joe said. "Believe me, it's important."

"Well, hell! I wasn't a-lookin' at his cock all the time. Hit's about average, I guess. Wasn't no real big 'un. Hell, I seen an A-rab onst had a dick looked like a flagpole. You could've hung your wash on that hard-on. Hell, I seen—"

"We get the point, Mr. Jones," Erica said.

"Bet them gals that A-rab socked hit to got the point, too!" He cackled.

"And after this man finished with the dead girl?" Joe asked.

"Stuck it back in his pants and left. That was all I seen."

"I'm going to have a police artist come by and see you, Mr. Jones," Joe said. "He'll put together what we call a composite drawing—with your help. After you take a shower."

"Do I git to stay here and sleep and eat?"

"That will be arranged, Mr. Jones."

"After you take your bath," Erica injected.

"Never seen such a damn jail!" The old man mumbled and groused.

2

"We've got to do something to protect our children, Howard," Dan Hartman said. "We've got to bring this man out into the open."

"And what then?" Howard whirled on his friend. "What then?" He practically screamed the words. "What are you all trying to do, get me indicted for murder—attempted murder, and God knows what else? And don't forget—you're all involved in this, all of you! You're accessories to attempted murder, and you men are just as guilty of rape as I am. I would suggest you remember that."

"Howard," Debbie said, "all that took place twenty-six years ago. Surely there are statutes of limitations to take care of all that?"

"This involves murder and rape," Bill Lewis said. "On theft, on a John Doe warrant, yes, seven years, I think. But not on a capital crime." He was thoughtful for a moment. "But Howard's right, we are all implicated. It's Paul," he said softly. "He's back, and taking his revenge, after all these years."

His soft words touched each man and woman in the room.

"But why our kids?" Debbie Harkins Mack asked. "Why take it out on our kids? Why not on us? We're the ones who did that thing that night."

"My dear," her husband said, slurring the words drunkenly, "Milton said it best, I believe—Revenge is a kind of wild justice, which the more man's nature—"

His wife glared at him. "Oh, Peter, shut your goddamn stupid mouth!"

Peter returned to his drinking, a smile on his lips. "Certainly, dear."

"Why our kids?" Steve Rick said. "That's easy. Because Judy was a kid when we did what we did to her. And so was Paul. That's why."

"Aw, come on, Steve," Jay Richard said. "Say the words—we raped her. All of us. We took turns." He began to cry. "Just like what happened to Laura." He put his face in his hands and openly wept.

The men turned away from the sight of their friend weeping. Steve thought of his daughter, Karen, a senior this year at Denton. Homecoming Queen. A beautiful girl. He shuddered at the thought of her becoming a statistic in a police department's murder file.

"But we were just kids!" Jude Stagg injected. "Just kids. Drunk kids, at that." He, too, had been thinking of his children, especially of his daughter, Aimee—cheerleader, and senior at Denton.

"Ah, yes." Peter's face brightened past its usual red flush from too much booze. "Youth is a blunder, manhood a struggle, old age a regret. So says Disraeli."

"Peter," his wife warned, "if you open that flapping mouth of yours one more time, I'll—"

"Better my mouth be perpetually open than your cunt," he told her. "Who, may I ask, is the lucky man this night?"

"Knock it off!" Howard yelled. "Fight at home, will you?" He looked around the room. "Jude is right, you know. We *were* just drunk kids that night."

"My God, Howard!" his wife blurted, unlike her. "You think that's an excuse? We were animals that night—all of us. I'd managed to forget it, as much as possible. Now it's thrown back in our faces. God is punishing us for what we did."

"Vengeance is mine, sayeth the Lord," Peter muttered.

His wife glared at him.

"Damn, Peter!" Marsha Kennedy said. "You're giving me the creeps."

Sissy put her face in her hands and began sobbing, her body shaking from her violent weeping.

"We've got to do something!" Lyle Barnett said. "I've got one daughter left, and I'm not going to have anything happen to her. God help me, I just don't know what I'd do if anything were to happen to Alice. We have to think of something!"

"How do you plan to prevent something happening to her?" he was asked.

"I don't know. Send her away. Hire a bodyguard. I just don't know."

"Hiring bodyguards won't help." Howard shook his head. "Not in the long run. I think Paul has been back for years, a part of the community. He's just been waiting for the kids to grow up. Hiring a bodyguard, or bodyguards, wouldn't stop him. He's managed to confuse an entire police force, including a lot of troopers. Paul would just slip back into his everyday role and wait it out."

"Then what do we do?" he was asked.

Howard shook his head. "I don't know."

3

"Oh, hi." Aimee Stagg opened the door to greet Father Cary. The night lay heavy behind him, blending in with his dark clothes.

"How are you, Aimee?"

"Fine, Father. If you're looking for Daddy and Mother, they went over to the Jordan house for something. Would you like to come in and wait for them? They shouldn't be too much longer."

"How much longer, Aimee?"

"Oh, 'bout half an hour or so."

He nodded his head. "Then I'll wait, if you don't mind."

"Sure. Come on in. I'll go fix you a cup of coffee."

"That would be nice," the soft-spoken priest said, stepping into the mansion. The door closed behind him. "For I'm afraid I have some bad news."

"Oh? Well, let me get your coffee and you can tell me first."

She turned her back to him and he reached for her.

* * *

Erica walked into Joe's office at the station house. They were both working late. "Father Cary was nowhere to be found last night. A couple of my friends are Catholic, and went to see him. The rectory was buttoned up tight."

"What time was this?"

"They first tried to see him around eight. They quit trying just before midnight. They'd been having a little marital problem and wanted to talk with him."

"Where is Father Cary now?"

"I can't find him. And there's this: Sheriff Roberts is up at the Jordan house again. That's every night this week. And, Joe?"

"Yeah?"

"I did a little more poking around on Father Cary."

"I could make something dirty out of that, babe." He grinned at her.

"Be serious. Father Cary is from California."

"Let's go."

"Oh, God!" the teenager cried. "Stop! It hurts, it hurts!"

"Scream, you whore of a whore!" The man lifted the heavy, metal-studded belt, bringing it down on her bare buttocks.

"Filth of Sodom and Gomorrah! Wicked bitch! Scream. No one can hear you. No one will help you." He tossed the belt aside. "Roll over on your back," he ordered.

The blindfolded girl complied, her body red and welted from the beating.

"Now," the man said, "you're going to entertain us. You are going to put on a show for us."

"What do you want?" she cried.

He took her hand and placed it between her legs. "Show us what you do when you're alone in your room, in your bed. Use your fingers, you naughty little girl."

"I don't do that!"

He dropped to his knees beside her and cruelly gripped her breasts, hurting her. He jammed stiffened fingers between her legs, penetrating her, bringing a wail of pain. "Don't lie to me, you bitch! You're the product of a whore and a bastard, and you'll do what I tell you to do. Don't lie. God will punish you for lying!"

Weeping, the teenager busied her fingers.

"You got the jacket on Father Cary?" Joe asked. They drove the streets, neither of them knowing exactly where to start looking for the priest.

The police radio hummed messages of no

importance to these detectives. Silent alarm at Foster's Jewelry. Family disturbance at 1010 Elm. Rowdy drunk at Bennie's Bar.

"As much as I could compile in a short time. He's thirty-nine, an orphan. Raised in a Catholic home in Sacramento, or rather, just outside of the city. College and seminary. Let's see," she flipped on the small lamp attached to the dashboard and opened a folder. "Cary's first assignment was an assistant pastorship in Ohio, and then to a church in St. Louis—no, the suburbs of St. Louis. After that, he came here."

The radio crackled. "All units in the vicinity of Hill Section. Disturbance at the Stagg home. Eleven seventy Crestline. Eleven seventy Crestline. Hysterical teenager reporting that Father Cary, Catholic priest in Denton, tried to attack her. She's locked herself in a bedroom."

The rest of the transmission was lost as Joe kicked on his siren, flipped on the flashing lights set in his grill and on his front bumper, and floorboarded the Mercury, slamming Erica back in the seat, the file folder spilling its contents onto the floor.

Joe and Erica were the first at the scene, burning rubber up the driveway to the elegant Colonial-style home. The found Father Cary sitting calmly on a couch in the living room. He pointed to the upstairs.

"She is up there," he said. "The child is

hysterical. There was a bug on her sweater, an ugly looking bug. I noticed it when she first opened the door to receive me. When she turned around, I reached for it. I suppose, with all the tragedy occurring in this community, she must have thought I was going to attack her. Miss, you'd better go up there and try to calm the girl."

Joe nodded his agreement and Erica took the winding stairs two at a time. Her voice drifted down as she called for Aimee to open the door. Other sheriff's patrol units began to scream up the driveway, and the house soon filled with cops. Then the highway patrol arrived, adding more confusion to the house in the presence of Sgt. Carter, who had been a Marine Corps DI for two years. He began shouting orders to his men, in a voice that could have been heard from one end of a parade field to the other.

"Oh, my," Father Cary said in a soft voice. "This does look bad for me, doesn't it?"

Joe smiled as the priest held out his fist and opened his hand. "The bug," he said quietly. "I thought it best to retain the culprit."

Sheriff Roberts stormed through the open front doors just as Erica came down the steps with the Stagg girl. After several moments of weeping and histrionics— which Joe saw through immediately—the girl apologized to all, especially to Father

Cary, who smiled and patted her on the shoulder. Then Aimee's parents roared up the drive and the commotion began anew.

"Stand back!" Carter roared, and the chandelier trembled and tinkled. "Make way for the parents, boys!"

"Jesus, Carter!" Joe muttered.

"Father Cary," Jude Stagg said, with more than a touch of rudeness in his voice, "just why did you come here tonight?"

The priest looked at the man, sadness in his dark eyes. More and more he was regretting ever becoming a priest. He was beginning to realize he was not cut out for this life. "To inform you of your father's death. He passed away about an hour ago at his home. Heart attack."

A deputy ran inside. "Sheriff? The Rick girl has just been reported missing."

"Roll it, boys!" Carter hollered, and the state police loped toward the open door.

"I have a headache," Father Cary confessed.

4

"The performance that Stagg girl gave tonight was Academy Award stuff," Erica observed. "What a terrible thing to do to Father Cary. I guess the rumors are true that she plans to study drama in college."

They drove toward the Rick home. "Yeah," Joe answered. "If he's innocent."

"Oh, Joe!"

"Come on, honey. We still don't know where he was last night, and I looked at the tires on his car. All new."

"You think . . . ?"

"I don't know what to think." And then Joe was silent, as a bit of local gossip settled in his brain.

Joe rubbed the back of his neck as tension tightened, then relaxed as Erica put her hand on his neck and gently massaged it.

"Think we have time to stop someplace and neck?" Joe kidded her, the tenseness vanishing.

"No," she teased him. "I'm waiting for you to have another argument with the sheriff."

"I heard that."

As at the Stagg home, Joe and Erica were the first to arrive at the Rick home, to talk with the girl's parents, Steve and Louise. The father was just barely coherent, the mother impossible to speak with. It was looking bad for Father Joseph Cary: Karen had been dating a Catholic boy, they had had a teenage spat, and she had gone to see Father Cary that afternoon. She had not been seen since.

Outside the Rick home, sitting in the car, Joe said, "Let's go see the DA."

***

"I'll call Judge Warren," DA Harold said. "I think we've got enough to pick him up."

Joe had isolated the bit of gossip that had been roaming around in his mind. "I wish you wouldn't call the judge," he said. "Not just yet."

All the eyes in the meeting room swung toward him. "Why?" the DA asked.

Joe sighed. "I just don't believe Father Cary had anything to do with these murders, that's all."

"Then why won't he tell us where he was the other night?" Sheriff Roberts asked, a bit put out with Joe.

Joe looked at him, thinking: *Why won't you tell me what you're doing up at the elder Jordan's house? What's going on, Sheriff? What have you got up your sleeve? And does it have anything to do with Paul Evans?*

"On the way over there," Erica said, "you said you didn't know if Cary was innocent, or not. Right?"

"Yeah, I did. But I just put some gossip all together in my mind. Some gossip I've been hearing, off and on, for the past year." He said no more.

"Are we going to play twenty questions, Joe?" the DA asked. "Dammit, if you've got something pertinent to this case, let's hear it. If not, let's call Judge Warren and have

Father Cary picked up. I don't like this, either. Father Cary is my priest, you know."

Sheriff Roberts leaned forward. "We've got nine confirmed murders, maybe ten after tonight. Spit it out."

"I think I can explain Father Cary's absence from time to time," Joe said quietly. "I think he's been seeing a woman up in Springfield. Been seeing her for over a year, so the street talk goes."

"But he's a priest!" the DA protested angrily. *"My* priest, to be precise."

"He's a human being," Joe retorted, "with human needs and desires." He looked at Erica. "Go pick up Father Cary. Just ask him if he'll come over here. I think he will, but read him his rights just in case."

She was back in half an hour, the priest in tow, looking a bit embarrassed. He had never been in a police station before.

"Sit down, Father Cary," Sheriff Roberts said. "Would you like some coffee?"

The priest nodded appreciatively. "Yes, that would be nice. Black, one sugar."

The sheriff looked at Erica, an unspoken command in his eyes: Get the coffee. She stared back, but made no move to rise. The sheriff sighed heavily, then got the priest his coffee.

"Relax, Father." Joe smiled at him. "I'm on your side. I think I know what's been going on."

The priest chuckled. "Yes, I'm afraid you probably do. Is this what the detective shows on TV call a good guy, bad guy interrogation?"

"Not quite, Father," the DA said.

"Father Cary," Joe said, leaning forward, elbows on the table, "you couldn't have had anything to do with the murder and rape of Laura Richard, could you?"

"*I* know I didn't," the priest said. "But how did you people arrive at that conclusion?"

"Because you were with a woman in Springfield, weren't you?"

The priest was rock-still for several seconds. He sighed, shaking his head. "Oh, dear. When did the cat get out of the bag?"

"There have been whispered rumors for over a year," Joe said. "Father, we're not here to fix blame or fault on your personal life. Believe that. We just want to clear you and get on with the investigation. Why don't you tell us about her, where you've been? And why all this aimless driving up and down in the Hill Section."

"I assure you, Father Cary," Sheriff Roberts said, "anything you say in this room will not leave here."

"You have our word on that," DA Harold said.

The priest and parishioner locked eyes. Father Cary smiled sadly. "You're disappointed in me, aren't you, Philip? Well, I can't blame you for that."

The DA smiled. "Let's just say I was shocked, at first, Father. But as Joe pointed out a few moments ago, we're all human. No, Father, I'm not disappointed in you."

"Well," the priest spoke softly, hesitantly, "as for the aimless driving . . . I was engaged in quite a bit of soul-searching. Driving is very relaxing to me. As for the woman . . . in my life." He smiled shyly, then began to speak.

At the conclusion, the men were clearing their throats and Erica had tears in her eyes.

The priest asked, "Will it be necessary for her to come forward and testify?"

"No." The DA grinned.

5

Karen Rick was found Monday morning by a fisherman. She was floating in a small stream. What was left of her. Her head was found a few moments after her body was pulled from the stream.

"God!" Erica said, then turned her head and vomited on the ground. "I'll be damned if I'll apologize for this," she said, wiping her mouth.

"Nobody asked you to," Joe said, looking at the body. A witness to all the depravity he felt man could commit upon man, he fought back hot bile. He could well understand why the fisherman had been taken to a local hospital, whooping and hollering in shock.

Karen had been horribly, sexually mutilated. Strange tracings had been carefully cut into her skin with a very sharp knife. Her body was covered with the bizarre markings.

"Get as many pictures of those drawings as you can," Joe told the police photographer. "As close as possible. I want them blown up. We have a psychiatrist coming down from St. Louis to help us on this. He may be able to give us a personality profile. So get in close, Al."

The photographer gulped a couple of times, then belched. "Thanks just a whole hell of a lot," he said, then went to work, his face pale.

"I'll put in a call to the station," Erica said. "The Rick family is Methodist, are they not?"

"Yeah, I think so. Tell the dispatcher to get hold of Phil Banning, the preacher. The Ricks are going to need him in the worst way."

Then he again remembered that woman that stayed on the fringes of his consciousness. She seemed always to look at him with a half-amused light in her eyes. What was it that made her so familiar to him? And why would she pop into his mind at a time like this?

Joe shook his head and pushed the woman's image from him. He had more important things to worry about.

He turned and Erica was at his side. "You looked deep in thought," she said.

"Yeah. I'll tell you about it sometime."

"The Ricks are on the way out here, now, Joe."

"What?"

"The press talked with the fisherman at the hospital. The family heard the news on the radio." She looked up at the sounds of a car fishtailing at high speed up the gravel road. The Rick family. "This is not going to be a very happy moment for any of us," she observed.

"I heard that." Joe's familiar reply was not unexpected.

The car slid to a stop.

"Get a blanket over that girl," Joe shouted. "A plastic bag, something!" Deputies began scrambling to re-cover the Rick girl.

But the deputies' frantic attempts to cover the girl came too late.

"Oh, my God in Heaven!" Reverend Banning exclaimed. The first civilian on the scene, he covered his mouth in a futile attempt to hold back the retching that surged up from his stomach. The minister gagged, his revulsion spraying the ground, triggering a rash of vomiters, including many police officers, veteran cops who had worked some of the worst wrecks in this part of the state.

Karen Rick's head lay several feet from her abused body, eyes wide in painful shock of slow death, bloody, tongueless mouth agape in a hideous grimace. Her breasts were gone, as was all sign of her pubic area.

Louise Rick took one look and began screaming, a long animal howl of shock and disbelief. She passed out, falling to the ground in a lifeless heap. Steve Rick collapsed in what appeared to be a seizure of some sort, jerking and thrashing on the ground.

"Goddamnit to hell!" Joe yelled, looking around the area. "Get the doctor over here and do something with this man. Where in the hell is that doctor?"

"Barfing behind a bush," a deputy replied, his face pale from all he had seen.

The paramedics assigned to the ambulance ran to the side of Steve Rick, controlling, or attempting to control, his convulsions.

"What a lash-up!" Erica said, knowing what Joe's reply would be. She was not disappointed.

"I heard that."

PAUL

I'm doing evil things! That thought roamed about within his brain. Paul paced the bedroom floor, thinking: I must stop it, fight it; must stop these awful acts of depravity. What I'm doing is wrong.

What you are doing is right, the woman corrected the man. You must continue until those responsible are dead. You must keep in your mind the awful things they did to you and to me. You must never forget that night.

I do remember. And I cannot forget. But sometimes, after it is over, I feel as if it was wrong.

Look at me, she commanded.

He looked, and she was naked on the bed, legs spread wide.

Come to me, she told him in a soothing voice. Come to me, and everything will be all right. I promise.

He came to her, crawled between her legs, and entered her wetness. He felt her arms around his neck and back, holding him. Her mouth clamped on to his, her tongue prodding his.

She whispered against his mouth. Tomorrow night, her voice penetrated his passion, we will enjoy ourselves with yet another. We'll make someone watch.

He was excited at that prospect, and she felt his hardness grow even thicker and stronger as the blood surged.

She said, We'll degrade and humiliate them.

Yes! But who?

She laughed wickedly as she wound her legs around his. And as if a partner in a perverted nightmare of passion, Paul came in the woman, his gush of fluid filling her, dampening the sweaty sheets. He rolled from her, to lie panting by her side.

In the darkened bedroom, in Denton.

Paul, and the woman he sometimes thought was Judy.

Later, they drove to the Rick home in the Hill Section, to offer their heartfelt sympathies and sincere condolences. She took a covered dish to Mrs. Rick.

It was the only decent thing to do in the face of such tragedy.

6

"And that's all you saw?" Joe asked the vagrant. "All you remember?"

"That's it, lieutenant. I don't know no more than what I done tole you."

The old man was bathed, shaved, and dressed in jeans and blue denim work shirt. He smelled much better. Unaccustomed to such cleanliness, he scratched at skin red from repeated scrubbing with strong soap.

"And you believe you'd recognize the man if you saw him again?"

"I think so, lieutenant. It was some dark in that old house, but I got me a pretty good look at the feller. He wasn't no little feller, neither. Even though I was a-layin' down, lookin' up at him, I could see him pretty well through the gloom." He shook his grizzled head. "I seen me a damn sight more than I wanted to see, I tell you that fer shore."

"I'm sure you did, Mr. Jones. Now, then, you would say the man was heavily muscled?"

"Yep. Carried that poor little thang lak she were a sack of Irish potatoes. And her bare ass jist a-shinin' in the moonlight through the broken winder. I could see hit all, believe me."

Joe laid a finished composite drawing of a man on the table. "Is this the man?"

The old vagrant recoiled back in horror at the sight. "Damn my eyes! Yes, that's him! Jesus Lord, that's him."

The picture showed a man of above average height, with powerful shoulders and arms. Long, shoulder-length hair. A rugged face with cruel mouth and lips, deep-set eyes, and thick neck.

Joe did not recognize the face. "You're certain this is the man?"

"As shore as I'm a-sittin here, Lieutenant. That's the feller."

"We'll have to keep you in protective custody, Mr. Jones. For your own safety."

"I wanna git the hell outta here!"

"Protective custody, Mr. Jones. We need you as a witness."

"Do I have to take any more baths?"

"Every day, Mr. Jones." Joe grinned.

"Shit!"

Wednesday afternoon.

"All right," Joe told a meeting of the task force, "let's count it all up and see what the score is to date."

Besides the task force, also present in the room were Sheriff Roberts, Doctor Williams, his assistant, Perkins, DA Harold, and a psychiatrist assigned to them by the governor. The psychiatrist, Jack Greene, was from St. Louis.

"Our boy is about six feet, maybe six one. A hundred and eighty pounds, give or take five pounds. Heavily muscled. he has long, shoulder-length hair, which is a wig he changes. Hair color, length—we all agree on that. He smokes a pipe. We've all talked this through and agree that he probably does smoke a pipe. He wears a size ten-C shoe, and according to our vagrant our boy is right-handed. Anybody have anything else to add?"

"What'd the lab have to say about the pipe tobacco?" a cop asked.

"So far, all they can tell us is that it's a blend," Joe answered with a grimace.

"Hell," the cop snorted in disgust. "Aren't most of them a blend?"

"Yeah, that's a lot of help, isn't it?"

"We got no prints on this dude," another detective mused aloud, "no samples of his real hair—nothing."

"That's it," Joe said.

"Well," a cop said, "I've got to go along with Joe's thought that this guy lives right here in Denton or Red Bay. Knows the area well, and most folks know him. I'd have to opt for a businessman."

There was a low murmur of agreement among the officers in the room.

The psychiatrist, who had been introduced to the task force before the meeting began, rose to his feet. "Lieutenant Davis? I'm afraid I've got to dash some cold water on this composite drawing. I've spent the last two days studying what is known of this man, and his victims. There have been cases of not only severe personality changes, but also of facial change, and sometimes the killer rapist doesn't even know he's undergoing these changes."

"Are you saying this guy may look one way on the street, as just a citizen, or at his place of business, and another way when he's committing these crimes?" Sheriff Roberts asked, disbelief in his voice.

"Yes. It's happened many times. You're all familiar with the recent trial in Florida, where the suspect had at least six very different facial expressions. An amazing ability to change at will."

"What about the cutting and the drawings on the Rick girl's skin?" he was asked.

The psychiatrist hesitated, then said, "A combination of emotions, including the desire to be caught, and of guilt. And of course, many others."

The officers looked at one another in disbelief.

The psychiatrist said, "After the body was cleaned, washed, I took a closer look at those cuttings and drawings." He walked to the podium and opened a large wooden easel, placing a packet of prints on the rack: huge, color blow-ups of the Rick girl. "Some of these still puzzle me," he admitted, "but still others are quite revealing as to this person's personality. And some are quite childlike."

"Keep this in words we can all understand, doc!" a detective called out. "We're just dumb cops, remember?"

The laughter quickly faded when the first color blow-up was revealed.

"This one," the psychiatrist said, removing the cover from the packet, and a couple of the younger deputies gagged at the sight, "is particularly fascinating to me. I had to study it quite closely. You all see these lines, six lines, with a slight gap in the center of the fourth line, second from the bottom? This puzzled me at first, but I am a student of the Chinese, and it soon came to me. This is a hexagram, possibly from the original I Ching, but it could be from some later translation—probably is, in fact. Could be from King Wen, or his son, the Duke of Chou, or it might be from Confucius. No matter, really. The symbol is known as Lü. It means treading carefully, such as treading on the tail of a tiger which doesn't bite the treader. Progress and success, no distress or failure.

"Now look at this photo . . ."

One young deputy left the room, gagging, his hand over his mouth.

". . . See all the broken lines? The solid lines stand for Yang—light, positive, active. The broken lines mean Yin, the opposite of Yang—dark, negative, passive. In Chinese philosophy, one cannot exist without the other.

"Now look at this one." He flipped to another blow-up. "This is crudely carved, but it is the number four hexagram in I Ching, known as youthful folly, or youthful inexperience. This is the most important of the hexagrams of the three, I believe. Perhaps, and I stress perhaps, this man is trying to tell us something that happened in his childhood, or young teens. But I don't know what, of course, and I must stress, it's merely a guess on my part."

Joe turned his head to stare at Sheriff Roberts. The man looked angry and upset.

Sitting next to the sheriff, Doctor Williams punched him in the ribs. "You ain't seen nothing yet, bud," the doctor whispered, smiling at Sheriff Roberts.

"Thanks," the sheriff muttered angrily.

Williams looked at him, curious as to why Roberts would be angry.

Then the doctor suddenly remembered who worked the Evans case, twenty-six years ago. He looked at Sheriff Roberts.

"This marking was almost missed," Dr. Greene said, showing a blow-up of Karen's genital area—or what was left of it. "Note the tiny initials, J.E., carved several inches below the navel. That, ladies and gentlemen, is a solid clue. Anyone here have any idea who J.E. might be?"

Joe smiled at Sheriff Roberts, who scowled in return. His face was pale.

"Doctor Greene," Erica said. "How many

personalities would you, ah, guesstimate our killer has?"

"I'm certain he has four very distinct personalities, probably more than that."

"And they are . . . ?" she asked.

"One. The personality he wears, exhibits, during his work day and social functions. The personality everyone knows him by. And I would say he is a well-liked man. I would venture to say some of you in this room know him, and like him. Perhaps you've been to parties with him, fished with him, been entertained in his home, and he in yours.

"Two. His sexual personality; he cannot enjoy any kind of normal—as we know it—sex life. I don't believe any of my colleagues would argue that point, taking into consideration his practice of necrophilia upon the Richards girl."

"Negro what?" a detective whispered to his buddy.

"Screw the dead chick," his friend returned the whisper.

"Three. I would have to call this his battle personality, where he changes his features, dons a wig, and commits his crimes of revenge, past persecution, whatever.

"Four. His personality where he fights within himself, knowing what he is doing is wrong, but unable, or unwilling to correct his behavior, to seek professional help. I would say he suffers flashbacks to his child-hood, mentally painful flashbacks. Whether these flashbacks are the root and cause of his behavior, or the, shall we say, 'good guy' part of his personality, I have no way of knowing at this time.'' Doctor Greene shrugged. "This is an interesting case, but by no means a first, I'm sorry to say.''

"You mentioned other personalities," Joe said. "What are they?''

"I would rather not comment at this time. I need to know more about the suspect.''

"If you knew who he was, say as a child," Joe blundered ahead, ignoring Sheriff Roberts's hot and angry look, "could you form other opinions?''

"Surely," Doctor Greene said. "Do you have information about this suspect that we aren't privy to?''

"Joe!" Sheriff Roberts uttered a short, one-word note of warning.

"Come on, sheriff!" Joe shouted his anger, startling the other detectives. "You know goddamn well who this nut is. How much evidence does it take?''

Roberts lunged to his feet, knocking over a metal chair in his haste. His face was ugly with hate and anger. "I warned you, Joe, time and again. This time you've gone too far. You're off the case.''

"Not until I hear what the man has to

say," the quiet voice came from the back of the room.

All heads turned. A youngish looking man with old, cold eyes had entered the room. Dressed expensively and very conservatively, he carried a slim attaché case. Something about his bearing exuded power.

"Who in the hell are you and what are you doing in this private meeting?" Sheriff Roberts asked, his face still red with rage and frustration. He banged his fist on the back of a chair. "Dammit, answer me!"

"Hello, Mike," Joe said, a smile creasing his lips. "Good to see you again."

Roberts spun to once again face Joe. "You two know each other?"

"His name is Mike Boyer," Erica said. "Works out of Jeff City—most of the time," she smiled.

Roberts slowly faced the woman. "How the hell do you know him?"

"I worked with him once, in Kansas City."

"Will somebody please tell me what is going on?" the psychiatrist asked, exasperated. "I thought this was a closed meeting of the task force."

He was ignored.

"What do you want?" Roberts asked the man.

"Let's just say there have been entirely too many murders and rapes in this area, sheriff. Certain—ah—parties—would very much like to see them cleared up. Immediately."

"Those the governor's words?" Roberts asked, his hands knuckle-white as he gripped the back of a steel chair.

The young/old man smiled for the first time—from his mouth, not through his flinty eyes. "I would not want to say that, sheriff. Since I really don't represent the governor's office—per se—but I am quite certain you get the drift of things. Don't you?"

"This is a local matter," Roberts replied.

"You asked for the help of the state police," the man retorted. "That makes it state business."

"Well, the state police can get out!" Roberts blurted. "We'll handle it locally."

"This is a resort area," the man replied calmly. "One of the most lucrative in the state. There has been entirely too much adverse publicity surrounding these murders and rapes." He maintained his tight smile. "It could cost this area millions of dollars were it to continue. And no one wants that to happen, do they, sheriff?"

"I've been in the governor's office many times," Roberts said. "How come I've never seen you before now?"

That tight smile. "Why don't we just say I keep a very low profile—until needed."

"In other words, you're the governor's hatchet man!" Roberts spat the words.

"Oh, I certainly wouldn't want *that* title hung on me!" Mike's smile faded. "Besides, how could I be? I'm civil service."

"Well, why don't you come over here and show me some identification?" Roberts asked.

"Of course. Would you care to see my ID from the state police, governor's staff, department of tourism, state park service, or the bureau of commerce and industry? You may take your choice. I can supply any or all of them, and I assure you, they are all perfectly valid." His smile returned. "Now, then, sheriff, which will it be?"

Sheriff Roberts sat down heavily, defeated, with a look no one in the room really understood.

Mike fixed his gaze on Joe. "You have a theory about this case, lieutenant?"

"I sure do."

"Then I'd like to hear it."

"So would I," Doctor Greene said.

"I heard that," Erica muttered.

Seven

To the disgust of the officers, and Mike Boyer's amusement, Sheriff Roberts swore them all to secrecy before he would allow Joe to say anything. Then Joe talked for fifteen minutes, outlining in detail his theory on Paul and Judy Evans and what was happening in Denton and Red Bay because of the events of that summer night, twenty-six years ago.

"I'll buy your theory," Mike said.

"Yes," the St. Louis psychiatrist agreed. "Everything fits." He looked at Sheriff Roberts. "Why are you—were you—so opposed to pursuing this line of investigation?"

Mike Boyer allowed himself a tight smile.

Sheriff Roberts said nothing.

"I'm beginning to smell a rat around here," Joe said.

Sheriff Roberts glared at him.

"We monitored your teletype transmissions and returns the other day, Joe," Mike said. "After that, I sent a man in here to, ah, test the waters, so to speak. He couldn't pick up any sign of this department following up on those obvious moves of the boy with a head wound. I wondered why not."

"What the hell are you?" Roberts said angrily. "A goddamn spy from Jeff City?"

He was ignored.

Mike continued, "I talked with Sergeant Carter of the state police. He could not understand why your theory was not being followed through, if only to tie up another dead end should it prove incorrect. So I then dropped what I was working on and did some investigating of my own. I found some rather interesting aspects to this case. They date back some twenty-six years, and caused the hairs on my neck to prickle a bit."

Sheriff Roberts rose to his feet, his hands balled into fists. He was trembling. "Mister," he said through clenched teeth, "you damn well better be able to prove any allegations."

"Have I made any, sheriff?" Mike asked innocently.

The sheriff sat down.

"Joe," Mike shifted his gaze, "I know you've kept records on the Evans case. When we had a few drinks in St. Louis several years ago, you mentioned just enough about them to arouse my interest. I kept what you told me that night in the back of my mind, and when this case came up I did a bit of digging, and kept what I found to myself. When this case began bogging down, despite all your facts and suppositions, I did a little more digging. Who was the deputy who worked the Evans case, Joe?"

Joe shrugged his shoulders. "I don't know. When we moved from the old office building—years ago—some files were lost. Part of the Evans file among them. I tried to find out who worked the case, but I never could."

The state investigator looked at Sheriff Roberts. The man seemed to shrink a bit, and looked suddenly old. He refused to meet Boyer's eyes.

Mike said, "Care to elaborate on the Evans case, sheriff?"

"You know it all, I suppose," the sheriff said in a voice no louder than a whisper. "Why don't you run your mouth a while longer?"

"A young deputy named Thomas Langford Roberts worked the case," Mike said. He had not moved from his spot in the rear of the meeting room—the War Room, as it is called by cops. "At age thirty, the man became sheriff of Morrison County, backed by big money. I believe that big money is called the Elite Eleven in this county."

"You'd better be able to prove all this," the sheriff warned in a quiet voice.

"I can," Mike assured him. "And a lot more. Do you want to discuss all this in private, or air all your dirty linen in public?"

"I don't care what you do, or what you say," Roberts replied in his unusually quiet tone. "Most of it is going to be supposition, and you know that. The statute of limitations—if you can prove *any* of what you say, and I doubt that—will take care of the rest of it."

For the first time that evening, Mike was puzzled, his face mirroring the bafflement. "I don't understand you, Roberts. You really don't care?"

"No. I really don't care—not anymore. I'm just tired of it. First, Old Man Jordan wants Joe on the case. Then he changes his mind and wants him off. He's been runnin' me ragged up and down the Hill Section."

"When he saw where the investigation was leading?" Mike asked.

The sheriff shrugged. "You're putting the hypothesis together, hotshot. You tell me."

"But you refused to take Joe off the case," Mike persisted. "Why?"

"I began to realize that I'm still a cop, Mr. Boyer. Or whatever in the hell your name and real occupation may be. Or family lineage," he added.

Mike smiled. "Let's just say you wear a

badge, Roberts. You're certainly not much of a cop."

Sheriff Roberts shrugged his indifference as to what Boyer thought.

"For the good of this department, and of Morrison County," Mike said, "I think you should resign."

The officers of the task force looked at Sheriff Roberts, as did Williams, Perkins, and Greene. The large room was abnormally quiet.

"And if I do submit my resignation?" Roberts asked.

"No charges brought," Boyer said. "And the press will never know what transpired in this room, this night. That's for the good of this department. Personally, I'd like to see you sent to prison."

That stung Roberts. He jerked his head up. "I don't believe you have any charges to bring!" he challenged.

"Try me," the man from Jeff City countered.

Roberts sighed, seeming to shrink in his clothing. "I've been a cop all my life," he said. "Since I was twenty-one years old. I made one mistake in all those years, and don't believe for a minute it hasn't haunted me." He looked around the room, at his officers. They turned their eyes away from him. Roberts smiled, a bitter smile. "May I go to my office and type out my resignation?"

"By all means, Roberts," Mike said. "Please do."

Three minutes after Sheriff T. L. Roberts walked slowly out of the War Room, Roberts, fifty-years-old, a widower, sat in his chair, removed a .357 magnum from a desk drawer, and blew off half his head.

1

"The story released to the press is that the pressures of the job got to him," Mike said. He sat with Joe, Erica, Williams, and DA Harold. They were alone in the War Room.

"How about the other officers in the task force?" Joe asked.

"I've spoken with them," Mike shook his head. "They're pretty well disgusted with the entire matter. They'll keep their mouths shut long enough. Rumors will surface, in time. But they will be just that. Rumors."

Joe, Erica, Williams, and DA Harold all looked at one another.

"Don't worry," Mike assured them. "By the time I get through with this, and the killer rapist is caught, a rumor is all it will be.

"What can anyone prove?" He smiled. "Roberts is dead. I can prove Jordan paid off the Evans family, bought their silence. That money is taking care of the elder Evans in a mental institution. I can prove Roberts had a bank account of more than one hundred thousand dollars under an assumed name, in Kansas City. The interest from that money was fed into another bank account in St. Louis. It's a dummy corporation, set up by Jordan's legal beagles. And I can prove that solid, thereby causing Jordan a great deal of grief, maybe even prison time.

"No," Mike shook his head, "I believe—I *know*—Jordan and the other elder members of the money crowd in Morrison County will back off from this case, now letting the chips fall where they may. You're free to pursue your theory, Joe, and it's a good one. Paul Evans is your killer rapist."

"There will have to be an acting sheriff appointed," the DA reminded them.

"Word I get is that Joe can have it if he wants the job," Mike said.

To the surprise of no one, Joe flatly refused the job. "I don't want it. I'm a cop, not a politician. I'm opposed to electing law enforcement people, and my views on the subject are widely known. Law enforcement personnel should be chosen because of their ability to do a job, not because they're popular with the people. And my views will never change. I think Peterson in public affairs would make a good sheriff."

Mike smiled. "Peterson was the second choice, I believe, although I think you'd make a fine sheriff, Joe."

Joe shook his head, and the matter was ended.

"I always thought T.L. was arrow straight," DA Harold said. "This comes as a real shocker to me."

"The real pity is," Mike said, "as far as I can discover, he was straight. Roberts made only one mistake, and that was a quarter of a century ago. But he couldn't get away from it. The ramifications of that one mistake kept mushrooming on him. The money people of this county continued to hold that one illegal act over his head. That's why Howard Jordan and some of his buddies never came before a judge for their many screw-ups as young men. Jordan and his cronies kept Roberts as sheriff of Morrison County for years, with only token opposition. When this case popped up, the pressures on all of them—Roberts, especially—must have been fierce."

"But it wasn't just the elder Jordan?" Erica questioned.

"Oh, no! Not at all," Mike answered. "All of them were in on this point—and I can prove that. But what's the point?" He rose from his chair and stretched, his suit coat opening. The butt of an automatic was visible, in leather, attached to his belt. "You've got a free hand, now, Joe. When Peterson goes in as sheriff, he will be advised to leave you alone. And I assure you, he will."

Joe looked up at the man. "Mike, I've never really got it straight. Just who do you represent in this state?"

The youngish man with the old eyes smiled. "Lots of people would like to know that, Joe. For now, let's just say my department attempts to keep the eyes of justice blindfolded. In a legal manner, of course."

"How do I get in touch with you, Mike? Should I ever feel the need."

That smile again. "You don't, Joe. But I usually know what's going on around the state. I pop up at the oddest times."

2

The task force working on the Graduation Murders agreed to keep their mouths shut about Roberts. They felt it was the best thing. Not to protect Sheriff Roberts—although many of the men and women on the Morrison County Sheriff's Department still like the memory of the man—but to protect the integrity of the department.

They became a quiet shadow force within the community. In teams, working 'round the clock, utilizing modern computers and old-fashioned legwork, with Doctor Greene staying on, assisting them however and whenever he could, the task force began the job of elimination of suspects.

They began working on checking carefully those men—and women—who were new in the community; who had arrived over the past two years, then four years, finally working up to an eight-year period.

And they drew a blank on every name. Everyone checked out perfectly.

Using the tire impressions picked up behind the Barnett house, and those found just outside the park area, the teams worked on matching the impressions. Here again, they drew a blank. No two impressions matched.

It was a frustrating and tiring three days for the men and women of the task force. A time for the killer to strike; knowing he would, praying he wouldn't, but hoping all the while that when he did strike again, he would leave a solid clue for them to pounce upon.

3

Aimee Stagg, still feeling a bit foolish (but also experiencing no small amount of pride) from her performance of a few nights past, stepped out of her back door to pick some wildflowers to decorate the dinner table for the evening meal. She walked into the field behind their house, as she did every spring and summer, when the weather was good, and had done so for more than two years.

A pretty girl, and—were it not for her perpetually pouting mouth—a beautiful girl. Tall and blonde, with full, high breasts and hips that held promise for any male eye that gazed upon them. They did, often, and Aimee knew it.

In love with her ass, one man crudely put it.

In the pocket of the jeans, which she filled out nicely, and tightly, she carried the .22 caliber pistol her father had bought for her. She felt safe enough with the gun. They had practiced for two hours a day for the past five days, and Aimee had taken to the weapon with a natural eye for shooting. She could hit the target from twenty-five feet away—not often in the bull's-eye, but she did hit the target, somewhere, every time she fired.

On this Saturday, she walked farther into the field, close to the dark wooded area she had been warned to stay away from. She hummed a Madonna song as she gathered a brightly colored fistful of wildflowers. The small revolver was a comforting weight in her back pocket.

She did not notice the shadow just behind

her and to her right, following her in the darkness of the woods. Did not hear the man's heavy, drunken breathing. Could not see his eyes as they caressed her, undressed her, and took her.

Aimee noticed some particularly beautiful flowers blooming just at the wood's edge. She looked around her, could see nothing to alarm her, and stepped close to the woods to gather the flowers. An arm shot out, the heavy forearm clamping around her neck, pulling her into the gloom of the timber, choking off an outcry. The wildflowers scattered their multicolors on the grass and moss and dead twigs in the woods. She felt her blouse ripped from her, her bra torn open, young breasts swinging free, hard hands touching her skin, squeezing her, bruising her flesh. She tried to reach the pistol in her jeans, but the hammer caught in the denim just as a hard fist slammed into her stomach, doubling her over in pain. The fist struck her on the jaw, and Aimee's world spun in madly revolving colors of purple and red and black.

"Don't fight me, baby," a voice drifted through her pain and confusion. "I gotta have you. I just gotta have you. Don't fight me, and I'll make it feel good for you."

Her jeans and panties were ripped from her. Hard fingers explored her.

She came back to full reality as hardness

tore into her, hurting her. A hand over her mouth prevented her from screaming. She opened her eyes, waited for the fog to blow away, and her eyes widened in painful shock as she recognized the man between her spread-apart legs.

She bit hard into the palm of his hand, bringing a grunt of pain as he momentarily jerked his hand from her mouth and sharp teeth.

"You!" she gasped. "Mr. . . . !"

Her head exploded in pain as his fist slammed into her jaw. Through her spinning world, she heard his voice. "I don't want to hurt you. I just want you for a little while. Don't fight me and this will feel good. Doesn't this feel good, baby?"

He stuffed a handkerchief in her mouth, eased his thickness from her, and drove in.

Aimee endured his grunting and panting until she regained her strength and then tried to claw at his eyes. He hit her again with his fist, stunning her. She again tried to claw his eyes, and he clamped a big hand over her throat, choking her until her world darkened.

"Are you going to behave?" he asked, his breath stinking on her face.

She nodded, and he released his choking hold.

She gasped for air, and allowed him to continue the rape without resistance. She lay still, refusing to show any sign of emotion as he hunched on her.

"Come on, baby!" he urged her. "Show a little life. Move your ass a little bit. You can't tell me you don't like it. That's a lotta cock I'm puttin' in you."

She pressed the side of her face against the cool earth and grass and refused to reply. Her only response was a small trickle of tears running down her bruised face.

He finished in a hot gush of fluid and crawled to his knees between her outstretched legs. He studied her for a moment, and then, with a strangely gentle hand, caressed a breast.

"Gonna tell your daddy on me, aren't you, Aimee?"

She shook her head. "No," she sobbed. "I won't tell him. Just let me go. Please?"

"I wish I could, honey. I really wish I could." Then he reached for her throat.

4

"It's not the same man," Doctor Greene said, looking down at the body of Aimee Stagg. Her neck had been broken, her head twisted at a peculiar angle. "This is a case of pure, textbook rape. He may have broken her neck when she screamed, or he might have killed her because he knew she would tell what happened. But it is *not* the same man."

"Two rapists to deal with?" Erica asked. "Isn't one more than enough?"

"Tragedy has a way of bringing out all the crud," Joe reminded her, adding, "unfortunately."

Erica was silent for a moment, then said, "They have now all been touched. Every member of the Elite Eleven. I would say that it was over except for Doctor Greene maintaining this was not done by our killer."

"Garden variety rape," Doctor Greene rose from his squat beside the body of Aimee.

The police photographer finished his unpleasant work, loaded up his cameras, and started to walk away. He stopped, turning around. "I wish you guys would hurry up and catch this nut," he said. "I'm tired of taking pictures of pretty young girls—all dead!" He walked away.

"Almost in our own backyard." Jude Stagg's words drifted to Joe, Erica, and Doctor Greene. The father had tears in his eyes. Since the property belonged to the Stagg family, Joe had seen no way, short of force, to keep the family from the death scene, ugly as it was.

Joe walked to the man's side and took his arm, gently easing him away from the sight of the dead girl's blanket-covered body.

"Jude," he said, knowing he should keep his mouth shut, but prepared to blunder ahead nonetheless, "this was not the work of Paul Evans."

Jude Stagg's mouth opened and closed several times. His face reddened and he gulped for air, momentarily losing control of himself. "Wh—you—you've known all along that—" Then he found his composure and shut up.

Joe met the man's eyes in an unwavering gaze. "I've known all along that—what, Jude?"

Jude shook his head as iron composure grew stronger in him. "I—I'm afraid I don't know what you're talking about, Lieutenant Davis. Paul Evans?" He shook his head, pursing his lips. "I'm not familiar with that name. No, not at all. Now, if you'll excuse me, I must see to my wife."

Joe sensed movement by his side and looked at Erica. "Lying son of a bitch!" he said in a low voice.

"He just lost his only daughter, Joe," she gently reminded him. "Can't you ease off just a little?"

Joe watched Jude Stagg walk across the meadow to his house. "Aw, Erica, what's to be gained, now, by them maintaining their high-and-mighty show of innocence? It's a sham and you know it—they know it, we all know it. Since this rash of killings and rapes began, they've met at one or the other's home . . . how many times? Five, six, at least. That we know of. They've got to know that now that Sheriff Roberts is dead, their cover of protection is gone. Are the rich so pompous and arrogant they believe all others to be stupid?"

"In many instances, yes, Joe, I believe they do," she responded quietly.

Joe looked at the woman. "Then I feel sorry for them."

She returned his steady gaze. "Perhaps for most of them, yes, you do, Joe. But these around here, the Hill Section group, you hate them. Just be careful your hate doesn't consume you, honey."

Acting Sheriff Peterson walked up to them. "Joe? Open the gates and let the press in. The public has a right to know." He added, sarcastically, "You know?"

"I heard that," Joe replied.

PAUL

Sunday afternoon.

Marsha Kennedy and young Dan Hartman made it a baker's dozen for Paul. Paul danced around his basement as he forced the older woman and the teenage boy to perform acts of the ugliest depravity, while

Paul's "sister" cheered them on. She shrieked obscenities at them and trilled her joy when her "brother" mounted the woman, forcing muted howls of pain from her. The depravity continued into early evening, and then Paul began his acts of torture, with knives and chains. When the woman and the boy had been reduced to babbling bags of idiocy, from more pain than a human could possibly bear, he killed them and stuffed their bodies in a basement storage room, leaving them to rot.

Paul prayed that night, prayed to God for salvation and a lessening of his evil mission here on earth. He prayed while his "sister" laughed at him, saying her "brother" looked so silly on his knees in the bedroom. Then he beat her, and she loved him all the more for the beating. After the beating, as he lay sobbing on the carpet in the bedroom, in the house on the outskirts of town, the "sister" took the "brother" in her arms, and they made love.

Later that evening, Paul went to visit the home of a sick friend, to give comfort and aid, and to offer up a small prayer for the suffering in this world.

* * *

5

"The state police is sending in more men to help us," Erica said. "As it stands now, we're overwhelmed with helpful citizens and their tips."

"How many tips have we received so far?" Joe asked.

"Over a thousand. The highway cops will work on those. Or as many as they can, that is." She opened a folder and placed it on their common desk in Joe's office.

"Something?" he inquired.

"Maybe," she tapped the open folder. "I have it narrowed down to eight people. These eight. Here, you read the summations, see what you think. I'll go get us some coffee."

Sipping hot, strong coffee out of a mug labeled MIGHTY JOE DAVIS, SUPER DUPER INVESTIGATOR (the label was put there by an unknown officer, months back) Joe's eyes widened as he read the last page, the report on the last name of the eight.

"Jesus, Erica!"

"Everything fits in my mind. The man is perfect, I believe. He's the one I'd put my money on."

Joe shook his head suspiciously. "We have to go easy on this one—all you've got is supposition, not fact."

She smiled. "Now who's being cautious?"

Her smile was returned. Joe put his hand on the curve of her hip and felt sudden desire surge through him at the touch. And something else, as well: he knew, for the first time in his life, he had fallen in love, and he rather enjoyed the sensation he had read and heard so much about, but, until now had never experienced. He had searched his mind, his heart, and he was certain.

"Something on your mind?" Erica teased him.

Joe's expression turned serious, and then he smiled, faintly. Erica had told him once that when he tried to look especially serious he reminded her of a basset hound who had just been caught pee-peeing on the floor.

"Erica, in the midst of all this tragedy in our community, all the confusion and fear, I have something to tell you . . ."

A deputy stuck his head in the office. "Sorry to interrupt, gang, but Marsha Kennedy and young Dan Hartman have just been reported missing."

Harry Kennedy was Methodist, his wife Catholic, and the Hartman family was Baptist. All three men of the cloth were gathered at the Kennedy home, sitting and talking with members of the family when Joe and Erica arrived.

"I've got one left," Harry Kennedy said.

The man had tears in his eyes. "Why is all this happening to me?"

Joe, remembering Erica's words to ease off, resisted a very strong impulse to tell the man he had brought everything that was happening on himself, some twenty-five years back. But Joe kept his mouth shut and his opinions to himself. For now.

"It's the will of God," Reverend Ballard said. "There is a time for everything."

Ballard was a strange duck, Joe thought, remembering street talk about the man— that he was an introvert, and had a history of mental illness. He also remembered that a minister's name was among the eight Erica had listed.

"We don't know that *anything* has happened to them," Reverend Banning said quickly, giving the other minister a dark look. "I would suggest we wait and see before making any further rash statements."

"I have to ask some questions," Joe said. "I know it's a very bad time, but I have to ask them."

Before he could, the house filled up with members of the younger Elite Eleven, friends of the Hartmans and Kennedys. Looking at Sissy Jordan, both Erica and Joe could see she was not too far from coming unglued. Her face was pale and her hands were trembling.

There was a bruise on the side of Howard's face. Claw marks.

Joe whispered to Erica, "Ease Sissy away from the pack. See what you can get out of her. Be nice. Being married to Howard, she'll respond to any act of kindness."

Erica nodded and moved away, to Sissy's side.

Joe cleared his throat, loudly, and the room fell silent. "I have to ask some questions of Harry and Dan, people. So let's everybody just calm down."

Howard Jordan fixed him with an arrogant stare. "Davis, I really don't believe this is the time or place to be bothering these people with your authoritarian manner."

Joe met his stare, contempt in his cop's eyes, then said what he had longed to say for years. "Howard, I'm attempting to conduct an investigation. So, unless *I* say otherwise, shut your goddamn mouth and keep it shut!"

Debbie Mack looked at Joe, sudden interest in her hot eyes. Linda Lewis gasped, a hand going to her throat in a typical well-bred feminine gesture. Lyle Barnett allowed himself a tight smile. Howard Jordan flushed, but kept his mouth closed.

Peter Mack, drunk as usual, said, "Ah, Howard, art thou finally made tongue-tied by authority? If Shakespeare will forgive me for bastardizing his prose a bit."

"Oh, Peter!" his wife said. "Do you have to start that crap now?"

Joe, fighting to keep a smile from his lips, said, "I'll try to keep this as brief as possible, and I apologize to the ladies for my profanity. It's a time of strain for all of us. Harry, Dan, if you'll both come with me."

After getting what information they could, Joe and Erica left the house and rode back to the station. Erica said, "Sissy wants to say something, but she's got a lot of fear in her."

"Fear of what?"

"Her husband, I think. I think he beats her periodically. Notice she always wears long sleeved blouses or dresses? I saw some bruises on her arms, and one on her back when she bent over to pick up a comb she'd dropped. I think she dropped it purposely, wanted me to see the bruises."

"Did you notice what kind of bruises? Old, new, how wide they were?"

"The kind we saw on the dead girls. Looked like they were made with a belt or strap of some kind. Are you thinking what I'm thinking?"

"Probably. Howard had a claw mark on his face, and a recent bruise, too."

"Nothing would surprise me about

Howard. Incestuous bastard, among other things."

"It happens in the best of families, Joe."

"Don't we civil servants know it!"

"Think I'm wrong to include Howard's name on my list?" she asked.

"I never said you were wrong. But the problem is, which rapist is he?"

"That, is the big question, isn't it?"

"He expressed genuine grief at his daughter's death," Joe said, drumming his fingertips on the steering wheel. "I know. I was there."

"Sure," she said sarcastically. "His young pussy supply got cut off abruptly."

Joe gave her a startled look; he had never heard her use that word before. He returned his gaze to the highway stretching out before them. "Girl, you have a dirty mouth."

"Men like that disgust me!"

"I heard that," Joe replied.

PAUL

Summer in St. Louis, and she was slowly recovering from the massive injuries suffered in her accident. She had undergone the last of her plastic surgery on her face, and was healing nicely. The surgeon had asked her who she would like to look like, and she had responded, "Elizabeth Taylor."

He had laughed, saying he would do the best he could.

The woman with no name and new face and the volunteer social worker became friends, and they daily walked the hospital grounds, talking.

"Where are you from?" she had asked him.

He told her he had no idea, no knowledge at all who he was, where he came from. No memories at all from cradle to a train mirror.

She knew exactly what she was, who she was, what she had been, and she would have liked to forget it all. But her hate and the creeping sickness in her mind kept it all fresh in her brain. And as they drew closer, in conversation, she realized that he, too, suffered a mental illness—confirmed, when he told her he did.

When she asked him what his vocation was, she laughed at his reply, tempering her laughter with a touch of her hand to his cheek.

She sensed, at first, this gentle man's troubles, then, as they began to see each other daily, he began confiding in her. But really, in her line of work over the past ten years, she had seen every kind of man, and probably knew as much of human behavior as many beginning psychiatrists. In her twisted mind, she began formulating a plan—a horrible scheme of revenge. And this man, this troubled man with no past, would fit in with that plan nicely. But she would have to wait, wait until just the right moment to begin bringing him into that plan.

As he talked, bits of his past began returning, always at her gentle urgings. Upon her release from the hospital—with Paul shouldering the bills, which were huge—they married.

But as time went by, theirs became a confusing marriage: sometimes Paul felt she was his sister (something she worked toward, as more and more of his past unfolded), and one did not do some acts with one's sister. But she was gentle with him, and did things for him that sexually drove him wild.

Then, one summer afternoon, as he worked in the yard, in the suburbs of St. Louis, Paul tripped over a branch and fell heavily to the ground, striking his head. His wife rushed to his aid. When Paul opened his eyes, he did not see his wife. He was flung back in time, to a pleasant summer's night, by a lake, with music playing. And he heard his sister's cries for help and mercy from her attackers and tormentors.

Then, after all the years, he knew who he

was, and what he had to do, with the help
of his sister/wife.

6

"I've called the bureau," Joe said to Sheriff Peterson. "But this is still a local matter,
for the most part. Can't prove kidnapping
for ransom. Can't prove any crossing of state
lines. We're operating on a John Doe warrant. No minorities involved, can't prove
any civil rights violations. We're stuck with
the matter."

The sheriff snorted derisively. "Killing
doesn't violate civil rights?" he asked with a
grim smile. "It goddamn sure would violate
mine."

"The bureau has two kidnappings in Kansas City, some terrorist bombing in St. Louis,
some sort of investigation going on in Jeff
City, and Lord knows what else here in Missouri. Said if they could spare some men,
they'd send in some agents. I won't hold my
breath. But Wainwright said he's given us
top priority use of his computers. All we
have to do is punch in. Military, too, if we
need them." He smiled at the acting sheriff.
"Remember, I was ASA. It's nice to have
friends that still remember."

"Without taking anything from the bureau," Erica said, "I'd like to know what they would do that we couldn't, or haven't."

"Probably nothing," Joe replied. "Except maybe give us some new ideas to kick around." He stood up, stretching until his joints popped and his tense muscles protested. "Well, gang, let's take what we have, bring it all up to date, add it up, and then travel to Springfield and feed it into the computer there."

"What the hell does that mean?" Joe asked, reading words in the green glow of the screen's printout.

The computer operator smiled. "It means the computer doesn't know who your killer is."

"Big damn help," Joe grunted.

"More than you might realize at first glance," the operator said, defending his machines. "Let me tell you why: you had government permission to tie in with other computers, and that's rare." He looked at Erica and mentally licked his chops. "Here's what we have—from your original eight names, the computer—or, I should say, computers—rejected three, Dave Hicks, James Smith, and Willie Winston. Of the remaining five, they are doubtful, including your prime suspect, this H. Jordan. Howard Jordan."

"I don't believe it," Erica said.

"Neither do I," Joe agreed.

The operator shook his head. "Don't get discouraged. I haven't told you everything yet. But let's look at the facts as you people have compiled them, and let's include Jordan with the other three. Not one of them meet the physical characteristics of your suspect, not even with platform shoes and a padded build. Winston doesn't drive a car. Hell, he was in prison most of his life, never learned to drive. On two occasions, Dave Hicks has an ironclad alibi. That pretty well kicks him out. James Smith checks out one hundred percent clean. As for those remaining, including Dick Ballard, things look very doubtful as to their culpability in this case.

"Now then, as for Howard Jordan. He's an unsavory man, probably a wife beater. You two claim he had incestuous relations with his daughters." The operator shrugged. "Maybe so. But that doesn't make him a killer rapist. Just a very sorry human being."

"Wonderful," Joe said. "But you said you hadn't told us everything. It's good news, I hope?"

"I went on Morrison County time as soon as you called me yesterday," the computer operator said. "I started working as soon as I received your information. Remember I asked you to give me the names of eight people whom you thought were completely above suspicion, to match against the eight suspects? Okay. Well, look at this. I played around with them. Hell, this is fun! I've got tie-ins I never dreamed I'd have—government, bureau, military. This is hot stuff for a small town boy like me."

Erica and Joe laughed at his boyish pleasure at playing cops and robbers.

"Now, then," the operator said, controlling his glee long enough to get back to work. "I've been up here all night playing with this, and I believe I've got something. The computer banks linked, messed around with each other, playing footsie, and gave me this info—Social Security says something is out of whack with this name and number."

"That happens," Erica said. "Social Security got my number all balled up once."

"Yeah," Joe said. "And how many guys around the nation are named the same?"

"That's true." The operator smiled. "But this name was killed in an automobile accident, fifteen years ago."

Joe was silent for a time. Reflective, he chewed at his bottom lip. "Can you punch up this guy's service record?"

"Sure. Give me a minute to tie in. You've already got permission."

It was a priority request. His file was on the screen in a matter of minutes.

"Now what?" the operator asked.

"Find out where he went to high school."

Fresno, the screen glowed, giving the name of the school and the graduating class of the suspect.

"Erica, call the station and have them contact Fresno PD and have them verify all this. If they can," he added.

Joe and the computer operator drank cups of coffee out of paper cups for half an hour, discussing baseball, football, and sexy women—one of whom, said the computer operator, was Joe's partner, Erica. Joe's reply caused the computer operator to abruptly change the subject back to sports, of the baseball and football type.

Erica was breathless upon her return. "No such person by that name *ever* graduated from that high school," she informed the men.

"Can you run a check on this guy's wife?" Joe asked the computer operator.

"I'll need her maiden name."

"I'll get that," Erica said.

More coffee out of paper cups, more talk of sports.

Erica walked slowly back into the room a half hour later, a puzzled look on her face.

"What's wrong?" Joe asked.

"I distinctly remember this man saying

once that he was married in St. Louis. He was the guest speaker at a luncheon I attended."

"So?"

"He wasn't married in the state of Missouri."

"So he's shacking up," the operator said. "Lots of folks are doing that nowadays."

Joe and Erica gave each other tight smiles the computer operator did not understand.

"Did I say something wrong?" he asked, looking at the pair of cops.

"No. You said something right. Using her married name, see if you can find out anything about her," Joe said.

"That'll take some time."

"That's all we've got."

More waiting. More coffee out of paper cups, the coffee taste indistinguishable from the cups. Erica read a women's magazine. Joe paced the floor.

"No information available," the operator finally said, looking up from his main terminal bank, set among dozens of computers.

"None!?"

"Nope. Not a thing. No Social Security number, nothing. She's a non-person. Doesn't exist in any computer under that name."

"No credit cards of any type?"

"Nope. Sorry."

"All right," Joe said. "Run the husband

from the time he went in the service to the present. Or as much as possible."

"Will do."

In an hour, Joe and Erica had the full package on a person who had died more than fifteen years ago. Who had the Social Security number of a dead man; who had lied about his high school; who had been stationed in Taiwan and become a student of Chinese philosophy and history; who was an expert rifle shot; who was now married to a person who did not exist. Both of them now lived in Denton.

"I think we've got our boy," Joe said, awe in his voice as he watched the green glow of the screen."

"I heard that," Erica said.

Joe looked at her and smiled.

Eight

Erica was unusually silent on the drive back from Springfield to Denton. Several times Joe glanced at her, only to see her deep in thought, brow wrinkled in deep concentration.

"Joe," she finally said, "where is your sister buried?"

He glanced at her. "What an odd question. She isn't buried, babe—at least not to my knowledge. Her body was never found after she jumped."

Erica thought about that—and other things—for a few more miles. "She'd be what age now?"

"Almost forty-five. Where is all this leading?"

"I don't know, Joe. I just have a hunch. Will you be patient with me? Please?"

He nodded. "Sure."

"Do you know the exact date she jumped from that bridge?"

"Sure. On her birthday. June fifth."

Erica solemnly nodded her head and

changed the subject. When they returned to the station house, she was on the phone for the rest of the afternoon.

Tuesday afternoon.

"A full twenty-four hours without a rape or killing," Joe said as Erica strolled into his office. "Marvelous. And you're late. Where have you been all morning, getting your beauty sleep? Not that you need any," he hurriedly added.

"You'd better add that, buddy," she picked at him, looked around to see if anyone was watching them, then kissed him. She closed the door, sat down, and placed a folder on the desk. "I've been working. I have a few friends on the St. Louis PD, and they've been doing some legwork for me. Tying up a few loose ends."

He leaned back in his chair. "What kind of legwork? Hell, honey, we know who our boy is—now all we've got to do is prove it." He smiled. "Your legwork gonna help us do that?"

She sat down on a corner of his desk and Joe put a hand on her thigh. "Speaking of legs." He grinned.

"I'm serious, Joe." He removed his hand and his grin faded. "I want you to listen to me—okay? With a detective's open mind?"

"Shoot, babe."

"We talked this over last night—about going to the DA with what we have so far."

"Right, and we agreed to hold back for twenty-four hours because we can't prove a damn thing on our boy."

"If he *is* our boy."

"I heard that."

"Suppose we could add more supposition to what we have, really firm it all up, with revenge as the motive—not just with Paul, but with his wife."

"Interesting. Okay, I'm listening."

"You're not going to like it."

"It's a tough world, Erica. Fire when ready."

She opened the folder and began to read. "On the evening of June fifth, 1983, a woman was found beside the river road in St. Louis. She had internal injuries, both legs broken, one arm broken, and her face was smashed beyond recognition. She was taken to the nearest hospital and checked in as a Jane Doe. She claimed no knowledge as to who she was, or what had happened to her. Her status remained that way all through her stay in the hospital, including extensive plastic surgery to repair her face.

"The doctors found track marks on her arms and legs and concluded she was a drug user. Smack. Tests proved this. The woman kicked the habit while in the hospital.

"The woman, Jane Doe, became friends

with a volunteer social worker. He was the only one, and I mean, *only one,* she would talk with, confide in. All efforts by hospital psychiatrists to break through to her failed. The volunteer social worker assumed responsibility for her massive hospital bills. Shortly after her recovery and release from the hospital, they were married."

"Quite a story," Joe smiled. "Brings tears to my eyes. Someone should make a soap opera out of that tale. Now, Erica, what is the point of it?"

She did not return his smile, and her eyes were cool and serious. Joe felt a stirring in his guts.

Erica said, "The woman was tall and slender, with dark brown hair. She had obviously been a very attractive woman. She was approximately thirty-years-old."

Joe's smile was fading fast. He let his chair come forward with a squeak of protesting springs. "And . . . ?"

"The only article of jewelry she wore was a small heart-shaped ring on the third finger of her right hand. It was not a very expensive ring. It was the first thing she asked about. Seemed relieved when she learned it was in the drawer in her night stand."

Joe was pale, his hands trembling, as his mind brought back the image of that woman here in town. Everything was becoming clear in his mind. The ring on her right hand, third finger. All these years of seeing her, and not knowing who she was.

He said, "And there were initials engraved inside the ring, right?"

"To M.D. from J.D."

"I gave that ring to her when she was in the tenth grade." His voice was hoarse with emotion.

Erica said nothing as she watched the man battle silently for control of his emotions. She was certain he would be victorious, and he was. His face lost its unnatural paleness and regained color, but his big fists remained clenched, still on the desktop, like solid lumps of hurt.

When he spoke, his words were ice-tinged. "The St. Louis detective who worked the case back then?"

"He quit as soon as the case was put in the dead file, as soon as you were convinced your sister's body would never be found. He became head of security for Jordan Enterprises in Springfield. He retired from that position five years ago and moved to Arizona. He died last year of cancer. His wife had died some years before."

Joe met her cool eyes with anger in his own. "Tell me, Erica, where was Mr. Howard Jordan, Junior, the night my sister supposedly 'jumped' from that bridge?"

She sighed, wanting the story to unfold to its natural end, but afraid of what Joe might do. "In St. Louis. He was registered in a downtown hotel."

"How did you find that out?"

"From old police files. He was picked up for being drunk and disorderly."

"Quite a cover-up," Joe said softly, his big fists slowly unclenching. He relaxed in his chair. "Damn, that must have cost old man Jordan a bundle. He really must think that dipshit son of his is worth the moon and stars. Why can't parents ever see the truth?"

"You're not a parent, Joe, so you don't know the love a parent feels." She shrugged. "For that matter, neither do I." She looked at him and smiled. "Yet," she added, "just remember this—we can't prove a thing."

He nodded his head in agreement. "Yeah, I know. All right, finish it up. There has to be more."

"I believe Madge and her husband are living here in Denton. They've been here for years."

"The volunteer social worker, the man she married—or is living with—he's Paul Evans?"

"Yes."

"Being the type of man he is, in his particular vocation, I would have to believe they are really married."

"They are. They were married in Indiana." She tossed a copy of their marriage license on the desk.

Joe picked it up and glanced at it. He grunted. "Our boy married one Jane Smith." He sighed, turning the marriage license face down. "God!" he said.

Joe sat for several minutes in silence, slowly clenching and unclenching his fists. "You're a good cop, Erica," he said.

"Coming from you, thanks. But let's face facts, do we have any?"

"Madge was—so I'm told—a high class whore with the fix in with some members of the vice squad." His words were bitter. "I know for a fact she was never booked or mugged. She was too smart for that. She picked her johns well. The SLPD will have no prints on her. I don't see how we can prove it's her."

"You can face her, eyeball to eyeball."

"The sad thing is, Erica, I have, many times over the past years. Every time I saw that woman, something about her triggered a response in me. No." He shook his head. "Facing her again won't rattle her, shake her. She has to be insane, like Paul. And she's a part of what he's doing."

"We have to pick them up, Joe."

"I know." He rose from his chair. "Let's go see the DA."

* * *

1

District Attorney Harold shook his head in astonishment. "That's the damnedest story I've heard in more than twenty years of practicing law. But I have to believe it. Too much of it rings true."

"Do we get the warrant?" Erica asked.

The DA shook his head. "I don't know. I doubt it. Let's add it up and see what we've got. One. What crimes can we prove either of them have committed? Two. Can you prove the man you say is Paul Evans is the man responsible for the rapes and killings? Three. Can you prove the woman you claim is your sister—who, by the way, is legally dead—had anything to do with the killings and rapes?"

Both Joe and Erica shook their heads.

"There you have it." DA Harold spread his hands in a gesture of hopelessness.

"This is nuts!" Erica protested. "We *know* Paul is the person responsible for the killings and rapes. We *know* his wife is really Madge Davis. We *know* revenge is behind all the deaths."

"But can you prove it?" the DA asked gently, knowing the frustration both cops must be feeling. To be so close as to touch the killer, or killers, and yet be so helpless.

Again, they shook their heads. "Not to a

judge's satisfaction, I'm afraid," Joe admitted grudgingly.

The DA reached for the phone on his desk. "Let's call Doctor Greene in on this. See what he says."

"Fascinating," the doctor said, after listening to the story. "Man's capacity for revenge is boundless, is it not? Of course, they are both quite mad. Certifiably so, I'm sure."

"Can we do that?" Erica asked.

"Do what?" Doctor Greene looked at her.

"Certify them insane."

"I don't see how. We can't prove any of what you've just told me. Committing a person is a large and long process. The easiest way would be through a next of kin. But in this case, there is no next of kin."

"Maybe that's it," Joe said.

"What's it?" DA Harold asked.

"Paul Evans's father. He went off his nut a few years after his kids were killed. Right?"

"So?" Erica asked.

"He's in a cuckoo house not too far from here."

"I strongly protest the use of that word, 'cuckoo'!" Doctor Greene objected.

"So he's in a funny farm," Joe said.

"That's even worse!"

"What about Paul's father?" the DA

asked. "So he's in a banana factory? Excuse me, doctor. A mental institution. So what of it?"

"Let's go get him," Joe said. "Let him confront his son. See what happens."

The DA shook his head. "You've got a mean streak in you. No way. My God, the paperwork would take weeks. I don't believe a judge would ever sign the consent form."

"The moral aspect is appalling!" Doctor Greene voiced his opposition.

Joe almost lost his temper, fighting back his hot anger at the last possible second. Still, his anger was very much in evidence. "Well, dammit!" He slammed a hand on the desk. "What in the hell is left to us?"

The DA attempted to calm him. "Settle down, Joe. We all want this thing ended as quickly as possible. But it has to be done legally. Come on—you've been a cop for too many years. You know we have to go by the book. Any screw up and the case is tossed out.

"Look, your sister—if this woman is your sister—has committed no crime. None. It's not against the law to disappear. She had no insurance, so fraud is not involved. The man you claim is Paul Evans can plead no memory of his past. So he assumed a name when he was a teenager? So what? He had no past, no idea of who he really was—what laws did he break? And remember, he's been working under this name for years. He assumed it, probably, as a minor, and good God, you all know the difficulty in working around a juvenile crime, *if* he committed any crimes as a juvenile, and we sure as hell can't prove that he did.

"No, I think our best bet is to stake him out, quietly. Let him move, but under constant surveillance. Wait for him to trip himself."

But while the police sat talking with the DA and Doctor Greene, Paul Evans and his sister/wife had been gone for a full twenty-four hours.

But not gone far.

2

Howard Jordan walked from his office to his car, leaving work early this day, to keep a prearranged date with Debbie Mack. A date they had kept, whenever possible, for months. A little afternoon screwing at his lodge on the shores of Bell Lake. As usual, Debbie would be waiting, so hot her cunt almost sucked him in.

Howard did not, of course, know it, but Debbie was all through meeting him for an afternoon's sexual tête-à-tête. She had already been serviced that afternoon. For once in her life, she had taken more cock than she really wanted. She had been appeased, brutally. Pieces of here were scattered about the lodge floor, her blood splattered the walls and ceiling—the workings of a mad butcher and his equally mad assistant.

And Howie stepped right in the middle of the gore.

3

The first shift of the surveillance team radioed back to Joe. "I don't think either of them are at home," the cop said. "It's just too quiet. The garage doors are closed, so I can't tell if there's a car in it or not. But there is a pack of dogs digging around a basement window. They're really raisin' Cain tryin' to get in. They smell something in there they really want to get at."

"Just hold what you've got," Joe told him. "I'm on my way."

The house sat a full three hundred yards from the nearest neighbor's line; set back from the road, among a thick stand of trees.

"Is it my imagination," Erica said, "or is there something evil about this place?"

"I sense it, babe," Joe said softly. "That, and death."

They knocked on a neighbor's door. "They left yesterday," the woman told them. "I thought they was goin' on an outin' to the lake. Told me they was. They sure took some things with 'em. Look here, Joe Davis! Can't you people do something 'bout them yappin' dogs?"

"I can if you're making a formal complaint," Joe said. "Are you?"

"I sure am!"

"Then we'll check it out," Joe told her. "Thanks for your help, Mrs. Matthews."

"Joe," the old woman stopped him in his tracks.

"Ma'am?"

"Something funny 'bout those two. I never could put it into words; never noticed it 'til 'bout two months ago. But there was something queer 'bout them two. They just didn't act right, you know?"

"Yes, ma'am."

"Joe?"

"Ma'am?"

She smiled at him. "When you gonna get married, Joe—settle down?"

Erica suppressed a giggle. "Yeah, Joe," she asked him. "When *are* you going to get married?"

Joe walked through the yard, muttering. He told a uniformed officer, "Call the highway patrol. Get hold of Carter. Tell him to seal off the area. He knows what's going on.

I just spoke with him a few minutes ago. Give them a description of the car and check DMV for plates. I don't think they've gone out of the area."

The double garage doors were closed, but not locked. Joe swung them open. A half a dozen full sets of tires, already mounted on rims and aired, were stacked about one side of the garage.

"Now we know why the tire impressions never matched," Joe said.

"The big one?" Erica asked. "Kill as many as possible, then run?"

"No," he said slowly, "they'll kill, but neither of them is going to run." He would not elaborate further, even when she asked him to explain. His face was tight with tension.

He turned to a uniformed officer. "Call the DA. I want a search warrant to enter this house."

"You know he's gonna ask what grounds?"

"Tell him I believe the bodies of Marsha Kennedy and Dan Hartman Junior are in the basement of this house."

The young cop paled. "That's what I smelled when I did a walk-around, huh?"

"That's what you smelled. Move it!"

DA Philip Harold was at the scene in ten minutes, a signed search warrant in his hand. "I don't know if this will stand up in court," he said glumly.

"Fuck court!" Joe expressed his pent-up feelings, then kicked in the outside door to the basement.

"Whew!" the DA said, after taking a deep breath of the foul air swirling out of the basement. He put a handkerchief to his nose. "I know what that smell is. Brings back memories of Vietnam."

"Yeah," Joe replied, willing his stomach not to heave his lunch. "I heard that. Come on, let's take a trip into insanity."

"Sometimes I think I'll go back into private practice," the DA said.

The puffy, bloated, very unpleasant looking bodies of the young man and woman were found stacked in a small storeroom, sprawled obscenely in naked death. They had been tortured to death. Much to the relief of DA Harold, Joe closed the door to the death room, sparing him any more sight of the pair.

A half-full 55-gallon drum of water was found next to the inside steps of the basement.

Cautiously, they walked up the steps to the living quarters. There, they found a variety of sexual paraphernalia: instruments for bondage, S&M, dildos of various sizes, whips, chains.

"Did you two notice the elaborate sound-proofing in the basement?" Erica asked.

"Yeah," Joe said. "To muffle the scream-ing of the damned."

"Waxing poetic, Joe?" DA Harold asked.

"Whatever that means."

"Our boy was a real cutter, wasn't he?" the DA remarked, looking around the room.

"And so was my sister."

"Okay to use this phone?" the DA asked. Joe nodded.

Philip Harold dialed his office and asked to speak to one of his assistants. "I want a murder warrant issued," he ordered. "Then draw up others for rape and kidnap-ping. There will be more charges, but that'll do for now. The warrants are to be issued in the names of Reverend Phil Banning, and wife, Page."

Nine

"Station officers around the homes of the Elite Eleven," Joe radioed into the station. "Pull in every available officer and get those people under protection."

"Some people are raising the devil about the overtime we're putting in," the dispatcher reminded the lieutenant.

Joe's reply—long, loud, and extremely profane, while probably not a first on any police band—would surely set a record for vehemence.

Late afternoon, only two hours from dusk.

"My, my, Joe!" The dispatcher chuckled. "Such language from a civil servant. Shame on you."

"Anything new happened in the last few minutes?" Joe asked.

"Yeah. Debbie Mack reported missing. Howard Jordan, Junior, has not been seen since lunch."

"That one might go either way," Joe responded. The memory of what his sister used to be, and what she was now was very much on his mind. Also the bloody, puffy bodies of the two in the storage room. "They might be shacked up somewhere."

The dispatcher laughed. "Yeah, ten-four on that. Units rolling, Joe."

Howard Jordan was found by the highway patrol, sitting in his car, by the side of the road. He had blood on his hands, his trousers, and his shoes. He was in shock, the only sounds coming from his mouth a grunting, incomprehensible, "huh ha huh ha." A paramedic stuck an ampule of ammonium carbonate under Howard's nose and popped it, the odor bringing Howard back to reality for a few moments.

"She . . . ah . . . cut . . . huh . . . all to . . . ha . . . bits!" he managed to say. "Head . . . ha . . . gone. Huh . . . pieces all over . . . ha . . . the room." Then Howie completely lost his cool. And his lunch. Again. Eventually he would lose his mind.

Joe and Erica were at the highway scene in fifteen minutes, talking with Sergeant Carter of the MHP. They had passed the ambulance carrying the strapped-down Howard Jordan, Jr.

"If they're still in this area," Carter told the pair, "we'll get them. I got troopers coming in from all over the state, and Peterson is borrowing deputies from other counties. We're sealing this area off, Joe. Every road, every cowpath. The governor is sending in two companies of national guardsmen to assist us. We'll get them."

"How much sense could you get out of Howard?" Erica asked. "If any," she added sarcastically. She did not attempt to conceal her dislike of the man.

The big trooper shook his head. "Not much. I've seen people flip out before, but this one looks bad for Jordan. It took all of us to get the restraints on him. The paramedics took him to Denton's psychiatric ward. He's really flipped some bricks off his load."

"Let's get up to the lodge," Joe said.

"I am not looking forward to this," Carter admitted.

The scene inside the lodge by the lake was even worse than described by Howard Jordan. The walls were smeared with blood. PAUL and JUDY were crudely finger-traced in dark red on the walls. Debbie had literally been hacked to bits, then scattered about the huge house.

"Goddamn!" Carter exclaimed. "We'll have to pick her up with shovels and spoons!"

Erica excused herself and raced to a bathroom. The sounds of her being sick drifted through the empty lodge. Both Carter and Joe fought back waves of nausea. They knew her being sick was not a sign of weakness on her part, or because she was a woman. The veteran cops had just had more opportunity to witness brutality and blood.

Then she screamed hideously, a long, echoing shriek of shock and outrage.

Joe and Carter almost knocked themselves down attempting to reach the source of the screaming.

Erica pointed to the bathtub. "The other Jordan girl," she gasped. "I think."

Joe carefully eased back the shower curtain and fought valiantly to keep from puking.

He had once been asked, while speaking at a local high school, what was the main thing a cop should be able to do? Joe had responded, "Don't puke every time you feel like it."

He had not been asked back.

Fifteen-year-old Donna Jordan's head was in the center of the bathtub, grinning grotesquely as it sat in a thickening pool of blood.

Sergeant Carter's stomach rumbled beside Joe. The big man caught his breath. "Jesus Christ!"

Joe looked at Erica, taking in her pale face and large eyes. "You all right?"

"Just as soon as I get out of here," she replied shortly.

The men stepped aside to let her pass. "Phone the station," Joe told her. "Get the lab boys out here—and tell them to bring some rubber bags." He gently slid the plastic curtain forward, hiding the ugly sight in the tub.

"Thank you very much," Carter said.

"Don't thank me yet," Joe replied.

"Why?"

"Now we have to find the rest of her."

Carter's stomach rumbled again.

Part of the teenager's body was found in a closet in the master bedroom. The men discovered other parts of her scattered throughout the house. The strange cuttings found on the Rick girl's body were also evident on Donna's torso.

"Working traffic accidents is not very pleasant," Sergeant Carter observed, chewing an antacid tablet, "but it damn sure beats this." He offered Joe a stomach tablet. Joe shook his head. "Don't you ever think of changing jobs, Joe?"

"Every now and then," he admitted.

"Especially now?"

"I heard that, partner."

"Joe?" Erica called from the outside. The men walked to the small front porch, thankful to breathe clean air once again. They each took deep breaths and wiped sweaty faces with handkerchiefs.

"What's up?" Joe called across the expanse of carefully tended front yard.

"Howard Jordan, Senior, was just found in his garden. Dead. He'd been beaten to death with a tire iron."

Joe ran to his car and grabbed up the mike. "Double the guard around Sissy!" he ordered. "Don't let her out of your sight. She's the last Jordan left, and Paul will surely be after her."

"She wants to talk to you, Joe," the dispatcher's voice crackled. "Says she's tired of carrying this load of guilt around. Wants to get it off her back. Or words to that effect."

"On my way."

1

With her attorney present, Sissy Jordan told her twenty-six-year-old story of kids with too much money, of snobbery, of not enough parental supervision, finally getting to Paul and Judy, and that tragic night.

"You don't have to say a word, Sissy," her attorney advised her. "Really, I wish you wouldn't. It's for your own good. We need to talk privately."

Sissy shook her head. "No. No, it's time to talk. Just think of all the tragedy that could have been prevented had but one of us the courage to come forward. Well, I can't take any more of this."

Joe read her her rights with her attorney present, then started the tape rolling, recording the conversation.

"Who killed Judy Evans, Sissy?" he asked.

"We all did," she replied softly.

"Sissy!" her attorney sharply cut in. "I really must protest this—"

"Be quiet, Walter," she said. "Just let me tell my story as it happened. The truth, after a quarter of a century. God! A quarter of a century."

The attorney sighed and leaned back in his chair.

"Howard raped Aimee Stagg," she said. "And killed her. He came in the house that evening in a panic and told me what he'd done. He beat me into silence."

"Erica noticed the bruises," Joe told her.

"I meant for her to see them. Howard's been beating me for a long time," she admitted. "Gets his kicks that way, I suppose. He's really a very sick man, Joe. Mentally sick. Oh, don't misunderstand me. I'm not excusing or condoning what he did. Not at all."

"Let's get back to the party at the lake," Joe urged. "The night of Judy's death."

Sissy looked at Joe. "Even as a boy you

believed we had something to do with it, didn't you?"

Joe said nothing.

"You'll never know how hard Howard's father tried to keep you off the sheriff's department, Joe. But your qualifications were too good."

Joe remained silent. He knew very well how the elder Jordan had fought his placement with the sheriff's department. "The night of Judy's death," Joe prompted.

"We all got drunk and the boys raped her," Sissy said matter-of-factly. "All of them. They all took turns while the girls watched and giggled like the little shits we were." She smiled bitterly. "And still are, I suppose."

"Go on," Joe said.

"Howard beat her with a belt. Then we all struck her, but not like Howard did. He liked to hurt things. Animals, up to then. The judge should have had him committed as a boy, but his father wielded too much power, and got him off, time after time. Our system of justice is not perfect, Joe."

Tell me, Joe thought. *Tell me all about it, you spoiled little-big-girl.*

"Then," she said, "Howard began hurting people. Especially girls. He liked to hurt girls. Anyway, back to that—night. Judy managed to break away from the beating. She ran, tripped, fell down, and hit her head. I guess it must have broken her skull, or something, 'cause she went into convulsions and really scared us all. She died a short time later. To make sure, Howard smashed her head with a big rock.

"Paul had fallen, was tripped, I don't know, several times. He was very drunk—we forced him into much of that drunkenness. Then, we all agreed that with Judy dead, her brother had to die." She sighed heavily. "We all took a blood oath never to tell, then we all touched him."

"Touched who?" Joe asked.

"Paul. Then Howard agreed to—do it to him."

"Do what to him?" Joe asked.

"Kill him," her words were very soft and Joe adjusted the volume control on the cassette recorder. Sissy had aged badly in the past few weeks. She looked much older than her forty-three years.

She said, "We all dragged him down to the dockside, and then—Howard picked up a rock and smashed him on the head. Several times. Then we all went home. I never knew what Howard did with Paul's body. He wouldn't tell us. But when it was never found, I assumed he had put it on a truck or a train or something like that." She lifted her sad eyes to meet Joe's. "That's it. What charges will be filed against us?"

Joe shook his head. "I don't know. That

will be up to the DA." He turned off the recorder.

"Joe," she said, "don't you think we've all paid enough for that night?"

"Don't ask me, Sissy. Ask Paul."

2

Joe and Erica stood on the steps of the station house with Doctor Greene. A light mist fell, wetting the street, cooling the air. The trio stood in silence, watching the flow of traffic roll past.

Finally, Erica broke the silence. "What's he going to do now, doctor?"

"Kill," the psychiatrist replied shortly. "Until you catch him. And they want you to catch them now. But they are going to lead you on a merry, bloody chase until you do. That's off the record, folks."

"I have a hunch that neither of them is going to be taken alive," Joe ventured an opinion he had long held. He glanced at Doctor Greene. "Correct?"

"That would be my opinion, yes."

"Want to ride with us, doctor?" Joe asked.

The psychiatrist's smile was tight. "I thought you'd never ask."

* * *

"There is no way they can get out of this county," Acting Sheriff Peterson told the huge throng of press people. "Every road, and I mean *every road,* is sealed off. If they are still in this county—and we believe they are—we will catch them."

"How many men do you have working on this?" he was asked.

"About two hundred law enforcement personnel from this part of the state. Another two hundred civilian volunteers aiding them. We have two full companies of national guardsmen added to that."

"Sheriff Peterson, do you people have any idea where the pair might be hiding?"

"No," Peterson said quickly. "Not at this time. But the national guard is beginning a house-to-house search. We are closing the pincers gradually. They can't escape."

"Don't you think Lieutenant Davis should be pulled off this case?" a TV reporter asked him. "Since his sister is involved?"

"No, I don't," Peterson replied. "I most certainly do not. Joe is a professional law officer. He'll do what has to be done to bring this case to its conclusion."

"Suppose it comes down to shooting?"

"I hope that doesn't happen," Peterson said. Then he walked back into his office. The press conference was over.

* * *

3

Erica rode in the front seat, beside Joe, Doctor Greene in the back seat. The rain had not increased in intensity, remaining only a slight annoyance to drivers with the constant on and off of windshield wipers. The roads were slick, as the mist mingled with road grime, and Joe drove carefully.

"I have to compliment the citizens of this community," Doctor Greene spoke, genuine admiration in his voice. "They have shown remarkable restraint in dealing with this crisis situation."

"No vigilante action?" Joe questioned.

"Exactly," Doctor Greene said. "The anger is very evident in this community, but it has been held in check remarkably well."

"There is another reason for that, doctor," Erica said.

"Oh?" his voice sounded as though he, too, knew the reason, but wanted yet another opinion.

"The middle-class and lower-class picked up early on that they were in no danger. That the targets were the rich."

"Yes," he agreed. "A sense of relief from the majority."

"That's what I picked up," she said.

"Joe?" the doctor asked, "how do you feel?"

A minute shrug of his shoulders. "I feel okay, I guess. A little bit tired, is all."

"Have you faced the problem? Worked it all out in your mind? Or have you simply pushed it aside, planning to deal with it later?"

"What are you two talking about?" Erica asked.

"How I plan to deal with my sister," Joe said. "When I find her. And I will be the one to find her. Bet on that. Five will get you ten I'll be the one to deal with this . . . situation. Madge was always a schemer, a planner. I'll give good odds she hopes—plans—on me finding them."

"And on you doing what?" Erica asked.

"That's what got me concerned," Joe admitted, sadness in his voice. "I don't know whether she hopes I *won't* have the courage to pop a cap on her, or whether she wants me to be the one to end it."

"Doctor?" Erica glanced back at the psychiatrist.

He shook his head negatively. "I can't answer that question."

"But we'll know within the next twenty-four hours, won't we, Joe?" Erica said.

A half minute ticked past before Joe replied. "Yes, I'm afraid we will."

"Why are you two so certain things will reach a culmination in twenty-four hours?" Doctor Greene asked.

Joe met the doctor's eyes in the rearview mirror. "Because, in a few hours it will be June fifth. And that's the day Judy Evans was killed."

"And your sister's birthday," Erica said. "And the day she jumped, or, more likely, was thrown off that bridge in St. Louis."

"Yeah," Joe said softly. "And I have a hunch I'm going to have to give her a birthday present."

"She is mad," Doctor Greene reminded him. "And she's a murderess. You must keep that fact in your mind. Above all else, bear that fact in mind."

"Yes," he noted. "I'm trying. But most of all, I'm attempting to figure out what Madge would do."

"You don't believe they'll try anything tonight, do you, Joe?" Doctor Greene asked.

"No, I really don't believe they will. I think they're holed up somewhere, waiting. But I think tomorrow is going to be one bloody son of a bitch!"

The trio rode in silence for a few blocks, until Doctor Greene said, "Paul Evans, Reverend Phil Banning, was, I seem to recall, or is, an expert rifle shot. Correct?"

"Very much so," Joe said. "But we planned for that. The deputies guarding the suspected victims have all been issued flak-vests and ordered to keep a very low profile, just in case our boy—and girl—try some long-distance shooting."

They passed through several road blocks as they traveled the county roads, driving slowly through this part of Morrison County. All the deputies and national guard troops wore flak-vests.

"Heads up," Joe told them. "Stay out of sight until absolutely necessary. Don't take any foolish chances, and don't anybody try to be a hero."

At one o'clock in the morning, June fifth, Joe called it quits for that night, dropping Doctor Greene off at his motel. Joe and Erica went on to Joe's house and went to bed, falling asleep almost immediately, too exhausted to make love.

4

Over hot, strong coffee, on the morning of June fifth, Erica watched Joe as he laid aside his .38 Police Special and took a .41 magnum out of a wooden box. He carefully cleaned the powerful weapon, then loaded it with Teflon-coated cartridges. His face was strangely impassive, almost totally lacking any expression. His hands were calm, but his eyes were cold.

"Going bear hunting, honey?" she asked. She had fired both the .41 and the .44 mag, and both the powerful pistols had almost given her a nosebleed from the super-charged recoil and muzzle blast.

Without looking up from the pistol, he said, "I'm going to stop them when I find them."

She touched his shoulder. "That pistol will definitely do it," she said dryly.

"I heard that." He smiled.

A .41 mag, firing Teflon-coated slugs, will shoot through an automobile and still have more than enough power to kill a human being.

The mayors of Denton and Red Bay met with their councils and issued this state-ment: To all citizens: stay off the streets and roads unless absolutely necessary. Keep your children home and supervised at all times. We are in an emergency situation, so please cooperate with the police and guardsmen. End statement.

Of course, in any community, there are those types of people who object, for one reason or the other—usually selfish—to having their homes searched. Morrison County proved no exception. Judges were kept busy issuing search warrants, and the cops and guardsmen were kept on the de-fensive by bitter invectives hurled at them from some irate citizens. The massive search did turn up some very interesting items: five illegal, fully automatic M-16's; two Thompson sub-machine guns; four sawed-off shotguns; one .50 caliber machine gun (WW2 vintage), complete with a thousand rounds of belted ammo; a pound of cocaine; four hundred pounds of pot; one whorehouse that even Joe didn't know existed; a dozen people, married but not to each other, rousted out of beds; and one marathon poker game that had been going on for six days, with the participants wholly unaware of what was taking place in Morrison County.

The cops also discovered one city councilman who was a transvestite (caught him in complete drag); a teenage sex club involving fifteen- and sixteen-year-old girls (two guardsmen were later court-martialed for being AWOL and contributing to the delinquency of a minor; they failed to return to their unit for two days and it was a week before they quit smiling); four stills, and a cockfighting arena.

But Paul Evans, alias Reverend Phil Banning, and his wife, Madge Davis, alias Page Banning, were not to be found.

5

Joe gratefully entered the coolness of the station house at one o'clock that afternoon, wiping his forehead with a handkerchief and silently cursing his shirt as it clung to his back: an unexpected heat wave had blasted the area, sending the mercury into the nineties and turning the citizens surly.

The tourist influx was in full swing, hampering search efforts and creating a mass of confusion for the searchers.

Sheriff Peterson sat behind his desk, looking balefully at a quickly melting glass of ice tea. A half-eaten sandwich was pushed to one side. "They've slipped through our cordon," he glumly projected.

"No, they haven't," Joe stubbornly contradicted. "They're right under our noses."

"But where, goddamn it?" the harassed sheriff yelled, his anger not directed at Joe or Erica. The mayors of Red Bay and Denton had both been yammering at him to get results and ease the pressure; the press had pestered him whenever he dared leave the station house; his ulcer was acting up and he was out of stomach pills; and his wife had told him that if he ran for sheriff the next term she was leaving him, and taking her live-in mother with her.

Peterson had immediately gone down to the courthouse and paid his filing fee.

"Somebody in this town, and I mean, *this town*, knows about Paul and Madge," Joe reflected absently. "And that's where they are. That's where they're hiding. So where would they go? Where would a preacher go?"

"We've interviewed all their friends," Erica said, slightly irritating Joe because the hot weather had failed to muss her, mentally or physically. She looked like a million dollars. A ten.

"We're overlooking the obvious," Joe mused. "Walking all around it and not seeing it because we're so used to looking at it." He stood for a moment, then suddenly smiled. "Who is the team leader of section three?" he asked.

"A national guard sergeant named Dickon," Sheriff Peterson said, after checking a wall map. "Why? What's so special about section three?"

"If you were a preacher, a man of the cloth, and wanted a safe haven, sanctuary if you will—where would you go to find it?"

"The Catholic church," Erica said quietly.

"That's where they are!" Joe shouted. "Bet on it!" He was running out the door, shouting the words, Erica hard-pressed to match his stride.

Father Cary was found in a closet in the rectory, shaken but unhurt, trussed up like a pig, and gagged.

Joe admonished the man as he helped

him to his feet. "You did a very wrong thing, Padre. You should have called us."

"They asked for sanctuary, lieutenant," the priest's voice was calm. "I had no choice in the matter, not really. They said they wanted to talk with me. Then I could turn them in." He hung his head. "Foolishly, I believed him. Phil *is* a man of God, you know."

"He's also a murderer, a rapist, a masochist, and an all-around fruitcake!" Joe retorted angrily. "I oughta book you for aiding and abetting a felon!"

"As you wish," Father Cary said softly.

"Aw, forget it! Where did they go? Did they tell you? Give you any idea?"

"No. But when they left here, Phil managed to get into some of my clothes . . . and collar. And the woman found some of Sister Theresa's clothing and put that on. Sister Theresa is gone on vacation. The two left here dressed as priest and nun."

"Well, that's just wonderful!" Joe said. He looked at Erica. "Let's go find them and give them the last rites."

6

Dusk.

"Joe?" the editor of the Red Bay/Denton *Democrat* said. "Banning—Evans just called me. Wants to give me a statement."

"Where is he?"

"Didn't tell me, and that's the truth. I want a story, but I wouldn't lie to you to get it. Said he'd call back in half an hour."

"When he does, keep him on the line, keep him talking, interrupt as often as you think the traffic will bear. We've got to trace the call."

"Don't send any cops over here. That might scare him off."

"Don't tell me my business, Mack," Joe said. "He *wants me* to catch him."

"He's in the Alexander High School building, here in Denton," the technician from the telephone company said. "Main office."

Joe ran to the dispatch room and jerked up the mike. "All units—all units, police and national guard. Converge on Alexander High School, Pine and Clifton streets. Evac all civilians from homes around school and lay a cordon around the school. Don't make any moves until I get there."

A gnat would have had a difficult time penetrating the three-tiered ring around the high school. The outer ring was comprised of national guardsmen; the inner ring of highway patrolmen; the closest ring to the school made up of SWAT units, local and state. The press, local, state, and network, were kept in the background, the bright lights for the cameras forming a half moon around the school, the night punctuated by reporters' voices.

"It's a set-up, Joe," Erica said softly as they stood on the inner fringe of the third ring, a few feet away from the SWAT teams. "Evans knew the editor would call you, knew the phone would be tapped, and knew you'd come after them. They planned it that way, didn't they?"

"Yes, I know that," he replied, the weight of the big .41 heavy under his arm.

"They've got some sort of deadly game planned, haven't they?" Her face was tense, eyes wide with excitement and fear for Joe.

"That's the way I read it, babe."

"Madge wants you to kill them, doesn't she?"

Joe nodded.

Doctor Greene stood close by, listening.

Joe exhaled slowly. "When we were kids, Madge and me, little kids," Joe said, almost to himself, "we used to play a life and death sort of game. I guess you'd call it a game, I don't know. You know how a kid's imagination runs. Madge used to say if one of us came down with some terrible sickness— like terminal cancer, or something equally awful—the other would be duty-bound to put the other out of his or her misery. Some of our performances were quite dramatic, I assure you. I bet we came up with enough exotic illnesses to wipe out this state. Just as soon as I found out Banning's wife was Madge, I thought of that game we used to play."

"But you can't be certain either of them won't try to kill *you*," Doctor Greene reminded him. "Kid's game, or no kid's game."

"No." Joe's smile was sad, "I can't, can I?" He picked up a bullhorn. "Madge!" he called, his voice electronically magnified. "This is Joe. Give it up and come out. It's over."

"Hi, baby brother!" a woman's voice yelled from the confines of the dark school. There was an eerie quality to the voice, tinged with madness.

"You're not going in there," Sheriff Peterson said. Joe had not heard him walk up. "And that, pal, is a direct order."

"Hey, baby brother!" Madge called. "Remember the game we used to play when we were kids? Huh? Well, guess what game we get to play tonight?"

"I mean it," Peterson said. "The SWAT teams are going in, and that's that."

Joe's smile seemed out of place among the uniforms, guns, and teargas canisters. He shook his head. "No, sheriff, I don't think they are."

"What do you mean?"

"Wait, sheriff—those two in that school haven't played their final ace yet. I know my sister, and I've gotten to know Paul Evans over the past few weeks. They will have come up with something, some plan, to insure my coming in after them. And I want it to be that way. If somebody has to pop a cap on her, I'd rather it be me. Out of mercy, not anger or duty."

"Oh, baby brother!" Madge jeered. "We have someone with us. She's not having a very good time, either. Listen. I want you to hear something."

A painful scream ripped from the high school, cutting through the darkness and into the half-circle of artificial light. The scream of a frightened young girl.

"I told you," Joe said to Peterson.

"Who in the hell is that?" the sheriff questioned.

A metallic pop sounded as the school intercom and outside speakers came on. "That's Ruby Bradshaw, baby brother!" Madge called, her voice reverberating over the school and yard, echoing through the empty classrooms and dark halls.

"Ruby's fourteen-years-old," a deputy said. "Father works at the mill."

The young girl screamed again, long and loud. A wail of pure agony.

"Paul is doing things to her, baby brother," Madge laughed insanely. In the dark office, no one could see her wipe the drooling slobber from her mouth; her eyes shone rabidly. "They aren't very nice things, baby brother. Paul is a little bit kinky when it comes to sex."

Doctor Greene uttered a very unprofessional statement. "No shit!"

"Comes from his childhood, baby brother. Isn't that what the shrinks always say? Sure! Something was done to Paul by the good people of the Hill Section." She laughed wildly, then began to sing. A children's nursery rhyme. Hickory Dickory Dock. The mouse ran up the clock. "Paul's putting his mouse in Ruby, now, baby brother. Listen."

The young girl screamed hideously.

"Jesus Christ!" Joe heard Sergeant Carter say. "That broad's flipped her cork."

"A crude way of putting it," Doctor Greene muttered. "But basically correct."

Joe raised the bullhorn to his lips. "All right, Madge. What's the deal?"

"You, Joe. You, baby brother. You, sweetie," she called, her voice hollow sounding through the bell speakers outside the building. Her voice was rubbery, her lips wet with the slobber of madness. Paul laughed wickedly and began quoting from the Bible, his voice audible to those outside.

Madge said, "When you enter the building, Joe, through the front doors, I'll push

the kid out the window of the office. But the
doors have to be locked and then chained
behind you before the little cunt comes out.
That way, you're in for good, and the cops
won't rush us with you in here. All the other
doors are locked and chained, baby brother,
so once you're in—you're in. And, Joe, if
you give your word, I know you'll keep it.
You're so fuckin' straight you'd die before
you'd break your word. And, Joe, one more
little item—I'm gonna have a dog's choke
chain around this cunt's neck. It's pad-
locked in place and I've got it secured to a
bolted-down desk. She can squat on the outside of the building, but that's as far as she's
going. Any shooting from the cops, and she
runs a good risk of getting hit. But the walls
will protect her from any shooting inside
the school. You got all that, baby brother?"

Joe's smile was grim. He looked at Peterson. "I told you she'd have all bets covered."

The girl screamed in agony. Madge
laughed.

The sheriff cringed at the girl's howling.
He met Joe's gaze. "All right. But it's not an
order. I'm leaving it up to you."

"How 'bout us going in through the
rear?" a SWAT member asked.

"No," Joe said. "She'd kill the kid. Even
if you tossed gas in there, she'd still manage
to kill the girl. Bet on it." Joe raised the

bullhorn. "All right, Madge. I'm coming in."

Erica dumped a handful of .41 mag cartridges in Joe's back pocket. She kissed him on the lips, then stepped back into the shadows. "Break a leg," she whispered.

"I heard that," he returned the whisper.

With Erica's kiss still warm on his mouth, Joe stepped away from the protection of the cars and stood exposed in the harsh lights. He slowly walked up the sidewalk, his stomach tight with the anticipation of a hot slug ripping through his belly at any moment. He stood for a moment by the double doors leading into the hallway of the high school, his eyes darting left and right. The corridor was dark. He opened the door, stepped inside, then closed and locked the door. The sound echoed through the empty hall.

"Put the chain through the bars and clamp the padlock in place, baby brother," his sister's voice instructed him. "And do everything where I can see it." She laughed. "I'm watching you." She sang the words.

The madness in her voice caused a shiver to race up Joe's spine. He did as he was told. His hands were sweaty in the hot, stale air of the school, and he fumbled with the chain, dropping the padlock on the tile floor. As he bent to retrieve the padlock, he glanced through the office window and saw Madge watching him. Her face was pale, and although it was a face he'd seen hundreds of times in this area, he could not believe it was his sister's. But he knew it was.

She caught him looking at her and smiled her insane grin. "Hi, baby brother. Long time no see. Now, you just step away from the door and let me push this crybaby out the window. She's all upset, Joe, just lost her cherry—among other things. I don't believe she enjoys sex a bit." She laughed, her howling pounding in Joe's ears.

Joe touched the butt of his .41 mag, then pulled his hand away. He did not know where Paul was, and could not run the risk of possibly hitting the Bradshaw girl. And he did not know what other tricks or traps his sister might have planned in the event of any shooting.

The girl was naked, whimpering and crying. Madge slapped her, telling her to shut up.

The fact that Joe was contemplating shooting his sister did not enter into his thinking; for this woman, this thing, this creature, was not his sister—not the person he had known as a child. This person was a monster, nothing more. Madge was dead, dead after she was pushed from that bridge in St. Louis; pushed by Howard Jordan.

But he had to know for sure.

"Madge?" Joe called, and heard his voice drift outside through the speakers, and through the school, through the intercom. "For my sake, my information—who pushed you off that bridge in St. Louis?"

Again, that wild, insane laughter. He could see her hair flying, the drool on her lips. And it sickened him. "Why, baby brother, darling, I thought you'd have put it all together by now."

"I have, Madge. But I want you to tell me. I want to hear it from you."

"Howard Jordan," she said. "Little Howie. That kinky bastard!" And Joe knew it was going on the record, witnessed by at least two hundred people on the street around the high school. And it would be going on recording tapes from the press tape recorders.

"Why? Why did he push you? Why did he want to kill you?"

"Because I was blackmailing him, baby brother. I had him by the balls and was squeezing. Howard told me, one time, when he was drunk, that he killed Paul Evans, after he beat and raped Judy. He told me all about that scummy night by the lake. After a while, though, he got tired of paying me."

Something about her story fell flat, and Joe, with a cop's intuition, knew she was holding something back. "There's more—I know there is. Has to be. That isn't enough. Come on, tell me."

She sighed, then laughed. From the darkness of the hallway to his left, Joe heard a man's chuckle. Paul Evans.

"I had Howie's baby," Madge said. "A boy. Such a pretty baby, too." She began singing a nursery rhyme. Joe watched her cradle an invisible baby in her arms, rocking it, singing to the imaginary child.

"Where is it?"

"Here in my arms. Can't you see it? I named him for you. Pretty little baby Joey." She began to weep, tears running out of maddened eyes. "But little Joey is gone, now."

"Where is the child?"

"Dead." She sobbed. "Howie killed it. Smothered it one night with a pillow. Then he took our little baby away and buried it. I didn't see Howie for a long time after that. Then one night he came back, and tried to kill me."

"I'm sorry."

"You're not sorry at all!" she screamed at him, then began cursing him.

When she paused for breath, Joe said, "Madge, give it up. Let the Bradshaw girl loose and give all this up."

"*Nooo!*" she screamed. "No! I'm tired of all this talk. I want to play the game. The game—our game. You remember how we played the game, Joe?"

"I remember, Mrs. Banning."

"Ooohh, this is going to be such a fun

game, baby brother. I gather by your very disapproving tone, I'm no longer your sister. Is that it, baby brother?"

Joe did not reply; he was busy trying to find Paul in the darkness. Joe suddenly whirled about and ran around the corner, into the darkened corridor.

"Goddamn you!" his sister screamed, her voice leaping at him from the darkness. "Me, me, me! I'm the one you're after—you have to do me first."

A pistol barked and a slug slammed down the hallway. Joe ducked behind a trophy case. Madge was shooting at him. A small caliber handgun—.22 probably, from the sound of it, but a .22 will kill you just as dead as a .45. She fired again, the bullet striking a fire extinguisher hanging on the wall opposite the trophy case. Clouds of compressed liquid hissed from the long canister, creating an eerie fog that spread down the wall and along the floor.

"You cheated!" Madge squalled. "You're not playing the game fair. You're a cheater, cheater, cheater. And you're a sneak. You've been a bad boy, and now you have to be punished." Footsteps slid through the darkness of the hall. "Come on out, baby brother, and take your punishment."

"*Joe!*" Sheriff Peterson's voice boomed through a bullhorn. "Are you all right?"

"He's been a bad boy!" Madge returned

the shout. "Now he has to be punished. This is family business, cop, so stay the fuck out of it."

"Bad, bad, Joey," Madge said, her voice silky in the gloom of the hall, barely audible over the hissing of the bullet-punctured fire extinguisher. "I'm going to punish you, baby brother, just like the time I caught you with the little Barrow girl." She giggled.

Jesus! Joe thought, *what a memory.* Joe had been seven, and the Barrow girl six. They had been playing doctor and nurse, inspecting each others' bodies, when Madge had suddenly appeared in the doorway of the shed. The Barrow girl had taken off, hollering, naked, and Madge had blistered Joe's butt with a belt.

Joe remained behind the cabinet in a squat, silent, as Madge slipped closer, her feet making shuffling sounds on the tiled floor.

"Bad, bad." Her voice drifted through the murk of the hall. "I'm afraid you've forgotten how to play our game, so we won't play this game anymore. Ummm," she said, "let me think. What kind of game can we play?"

"We'll cut him up." Banning/Evans's voice came from behind Joe, and to his left. In a classroom. "Yes, let me have him, we'll have such fun listening to him scream for mercy."

"We'll both have him," Madge said. "For Joey must be punished. He's been bad. Ssoooo bad," she whispered as she slipped closer to Joe.

Joe realized then, and the knowledge hit him in the pit of the stomach, that there was only one way this game was to end. And he knew his sister had outsmarted him—again.

"Drop the gun, Madge," he said softly.

The trophy case he crouched behind was shattered from the force of bullets. The slugs whined off of metal trophies.

"Bad, bad!" she called. "Duty-bound. Now, baby brother, you have to do your duty, don't you?"

She laughed insanely and drew nearer. Joe could make out her shape in the darkness, and could see the pistol in her hand as she raised it.

She squeezed the trigger just as Joe threw himself away from the ruined cabinet. Flame and lead spat at him and reflex took over. Joe's right hand came up, finger squeezing the trigger, and the big .41 mag belched flame. Madge Davis Banning Evans slammed backward, then folded over as she hit the wall. She slid to the floor in a crumpled heap, her legs spread grotesquely, both hands holding her shattered stomach. She screamed once, then began a shuddering, macabre shaking as her life ebbed away.

"*Nooo!*" Banning/Evans screamed. He

threw his rifle at Joe and the stock struck the cop on the head, stunning him. Banning/Evans leaped across the hall to land on Joe, hard fists pounding the detective.

Joe took a solid shot to the chin, and his world spun. A shoe to the head almost put him out. He lay stunned, watching as Banning/Evans raised a pistol and pointed the muzzle at him.

"It's over, Paul," Joe whispered, his eyes never leaving the black hole of the muzzle. "Everyone has paid, in some form, for what happened that night, twenty-five years ago. Don't do this."

"You wouldn't play our game," Banning/Evans whined. "Judy was right. You have to be punished. Judy," he called. "Come help me. Don't leave me. I need you. Where are you?" His eyes flicked for just a second to the dark shape on the floor. "Get up. Get up! You look so silly on the floor."

"That isn't Judy," Joe said as he felt strength returning to him. "And she can't get up. Paul, that's not Judy. That's my sister, Madge."

"Liar!" Banning/Evans screamed. "Dirty, filthy liar! Now you have to die!"

Banning/Evans's head seemed to mushroom in front of Joe, then the sound of a shot came booming down the hall. Banning/Evans tumbled to the floor, the hole

in his head leaking his life away. Joe turned
his eyes to the shapely silhouette a dozen
yards down the dark hall.

"You sure need someone to look after
you, Joe," Erica said. She was crying as she
lowered her pistol, the muzzle still smoking.

"Yeah." Joe climbed wearily and painfully
to his feet. "I heard that."

Epilogue

It was breaking dawn, the first angry slash of the sun just peeking over the horizon, when Joe and Erica left the station house. The violent storm that had erupted just after the high school had been cleared had swept past, roaring eastward, cooling the land with its passage. Joe and Erica sat on the steps of the sheriff's department building.

"I love police work, Joe," she said. "But I don't *ever* want to go through another case like this one." She took his hand. "And if you say, 'I heard that,' I'll punch you right on the nose. I swear I will!"

"Hey!" the old vagrant hollered from the cell area on the second floor of the building. "Lemme out of here! I ain't takin' no more showers. I'm pink, dammit! Lemme out of this damned place. I wanna leave here. Is this a jail or a bathhouse?"

Both Joe and Erica chuckled. They had forgotten about the old vag.

"I wonder what will happen to Sissy, and all the others?" she asked.

"Probably nothing," Joe replied, but any bitterness he once felt was gone from his voice. "They very wealthy people, remember, and the crime is a quarter of a century old. They were all minors when it happened. Hell, a good lawyer can—and probably will—get them off."

"I think they've all paid enough, Joe." And she was startled to hear him agree with her.

"Sixteen members of the Elite Eleven dead," Joe said. "One in a nuthouse. The sheriff killed himself rather than face the public after what he'd done. Evans and Madge dead. Yeah, everyone's paid—including us—for this crime. We can close the book on it. God, it's past time."

"Joe? Not too many days ago, you started to say something to me. Something about in the midst of all this tragedy, all the fear and confusion—"

"Yeah, I remember. I was going to ask you to marry me."

"Yes!"

Joe sat stunned, looking at her, unable to believe her quick acceptance.

"Well?" she said. "Did you hear me?"

A slow smile spread over Joe's face. "Yeah," he grinned. "I *sure* heard that."

And she kissed him.

"Hey!" the old vagrant yelled from above them. "Ya'll go smooch somewhere's else. Git me outta here! Goddammit, it's bath time!"

CLASSIC HORROR

From William W. Johnstone